The man was flying by instinct

Nile Barrabas eased himself into the copilot's seat next to José Sanchez with care. The Puerto Rican pilot was fighting blackout every second and looked like he might not make it. As his eyes closed and his chin slumped on his chest again, Lee Hatton called to him, shook him by the shoulder. He opened his eyes for a few more seconds.

Barrabas had used flight simulators many years ago during military training. He'd had unusual reflexes and took to the stick like a natural. But he'd never gone beyond the simulated stage. He could fly the electronic plane like an expert, but he'd never done the real thing.

Suddenly, as they leveled off at about ten thousand feet, Sanchez slumped in his seat. The plane began to lose altitude, but they were still in Russian airspace, heading 180 degrees off course with an unconscious pilot at the controls.

SOBs
SOLDIERS OF BARRABAS

SAKHALIN BREAKOUT

JACK HILD

A GOLD EAGLE BOOK FROM
WORLDWIDE

TORONTO · NEW YORK · LONDON · PARIS
AMSTERDAM · STOCKHOLM · HAMBURG
ATHENS · MILAN · TOKYO · SYDNEY

First edition May 1987

ISBN 0-373-61618-X

Special thanks and acknowledgment to
Jack Garside for his contribution to this work.

Printed in Canada

1

United States Congressman Clint Weston was worried, and had been so for more than an hour. Once again he motioned for the chief steward and repeated his concern.

"I've taken this flight a half-dozen times. We should be passing east of the Kamchatka Peninsula, well out to sea. Dammit, man, there's no cloud cover. Any fool can see we're flying over land." He tried to keep his voice low as he pulled at the Korean's arm, easing the man into the empty seat beside him. "That's got to be Kamchatka down there," Weston said. "The Russians aren't fools. They forced one of your flights to land here five years ago and swore then that they'd shoot down any aircraft that strayed into their airspace again."

Weston's face, normally pale from too many hours spent indoors in Washington, was flushed with anger. He was a tall rangy man who had fought to the top the hard way. A veteran of Vietnam, a fighter pilot whose hobby was studying military aircraft, Weston knew what he was talking about. He knew that the Russians had fortified Kamchatka against invasion from the Pacific. If the Korean Airlines flight kept its present bearing, it would enter Sakhalin's airspace. As a member of the Armed Forces Appropriations Committee, Weston knew that Sakhalin Island was a hub of Soviet military activity. The army's modern aircraft and the most advanced naval craft were based there.

The Korean listened, but whether he took the congressman seriously or thought him a nuisance was a mystery.

"I have spoken to the captain, Congressman Weston. He has assured me that we are in no danger," he said. "The Russians know that we are a civilian aircraft." The man rose gradually to his feet as he spoke and then moved down the aisle.

Weston knew that they were well over the huge Russian peninsula by now. He stared out the window and down at the bleak Russian countryside. And then he saw it—a fighter plane raced toward them from the port side. It was a Foxhound A, a modified MIG-31. The Soviets had guarded their new fighter closely, but Weston knew that it could easily outfly the Korean 747. The Congressman also knew that the fighter plane was likely armed with eight AA-9 radar-homing air-to-air missiles.

Clint Weston sat in row number one of the big plane. Full-sized ports ringed the nose section, allowing Weston a clear view of about a hundred degrees. The Foxhound cut speed, signaled for the pilot to turn to port, dipped its wings three times and turned, expecting the passenger plane to follow. The Korean plane maintained course.

By now the other passengers were alarmed, something that Weston had tried to avoid. He pressed his call button, and the steward appeared, his square, expressionless face a mask.

"That aircraft signaled us to turn to port. Why are we not complying?" Weston asked.

"The captain has assured me—" the Korean began.

"Dammit, man, I know this aircraft!" Weston tried to keep his voice down, but it was impossible. "If it strays off course, computerized navigational equipment takes over. Dammit, this plane has three fail-safe computer mechanisms to make sure that doesn't happen. Obviously we are on a programmed course. The captain's endangering the lives of everyone on board."

Weston had had enough. He got up, pushed past the steward and headed for the curved staircase and the upper deck. He'd have this out with the captain himself.

GEORGE EASTMAN HAD WATCHED the Russian fighter from his window seat at the rear of the 747. The former Canadian bush pilot was one of the 250 passengers in tourist class. Everyone on the plane was now visibly upset. Some women cried, while others comforted small children.

The Foxhound, the monstrous military plane with its dual tail fins and eight rockets, had long since disappeared. The 747 had flown over water again, and Eastman watched as land reappeared under the starboard wing. He knew his geography. It had to be

Sakhalin Island, one of Russia's most fortified territories. George Eastman began to sweat.

As if on cue, a second aircraft pulled to the port side of the 747. It was a U-15, a standard Soviet Fighter that could fly three times the speed of the 747. A chill raced down Eastman's spine when he noted the two heat-seeking rockets slung under its wings.

The Soviet pilot signaled the plane to change course, but again the Korean pilot ignored the request. The planes left Sakhalin behind and approached La Pérouse Strait, a forty-mile channel separating Russia from Japan.

Eastman began to relax as he watched the fighter draw back and disappear from view. He flipped a cigarette from his pack and was about to light it when a roaring sound approached from the rear.

The 747 rocked as one engine exploded in flames, taking most of the starboard wing with it. Gasoline from the wing flamed along the fuselage past the window opposite him. A second explosion roared in his ears as another rocket took out a port-side engine. Flame engulfed the other side of the fuselage.

Screams of horror filled the cabin. The flames didn't last long but covered the windows with black sludge, turning the cabin into a dark coffin. The plane began its plunge toward the sea.

George Eastman was strapped to his seat as the 269 passengers and crew began the long plunge to death.

Those who had jumped from their seats fell forward, smashing into bulkheads, and coming to a rest against the galley wall.

In the midst of horror, the screams and the prayers, Eastman thought about life—how full it had been. Strangely, he wasn't scared.

CLINT WESTON KNEW that he was going to die. The pilot of the U-15 had given the captain all the warning he deserved. Weston was aware of what the Russians were protecting below. As the U-15 dropped back, he knew exactly what would be transpiring between the fighter aircraft and its control tower.

Soviet ground control: "Take aim at the target."
U-15 pilot: "Aim Taken."
Ground control: "Fire."
Pilot: "Fired."

Weston sat back in his seat. He thought of his wife and kids, of the triumphs and disappointments that he would not be there to share with them.

Then he heard it. Only for a fraction of a second, but he heard it—the whoosh of a rocket as it caught up to, and slammed into a starboard engine of, the Korean airliner. He couldn't see the flash of fire from his seat, but he felt the concussion, felt the aircraft shudder in the beginning of its death throe.

A second explosion, this time on the port side. He saw the engine disintegrate and the flames pour out of ruptured wing tanks, engulfing those in the rear. He could see clearly out the forward ports. The nose of the silver bird dipped to a thirty-degree angle of descent...then forty...then sixty.

They were plunging out of control from thirty-five thousand feet. How long would it take? How much of life was left? As he asked the question, a crushing weight pinned him to the forward hull as the seat behind him broke from the floor mounts.

It was becoming harder to catch his breath as the weight increased. A body crashed next to his head. Trapped and crushed, he felt blood from a smashed skull gush over his face. It wouldn't make any difference. Green spots formed behind his eyelids—dancing spots—green turning to gray and finally to black.

Clint Weston had not wanted to die. He'd wanted the chance to do things differently.

Few people get a second chance.

2

They hadn't seen a cloud for a week. Penang, an island off the coast of Malaysia, was known as "the Pearl of the Orient." It deserved its name. The island was sun-drenched, surrounded by beaches and populated by friendly people. They walked the beach every morning, lay by the hotel's magnificent pool every afternoon, made love before dinner and slept soundly every night, wrapped in each other's arms.

It was unusual for the man to lie idle, to soak up the sun, but the last job had exhausted him. He was finally spending time with his lover, a woman whom he saw less often than he would like.

He lay on his stomach on the lounger, his head resting on one arm, looking at her. She lay beside him, her black bikini covering very little, leaving the beautifully sculpted body on display for all to see. It seemed to the man beside her that every man in the hotel walked out of his way to draw near his woman. She had taken off her top, and when she rolled to her back, shading her eyes with one hand, she became the center of everyone's attention.

Not all of those who drifted by the two sunbathers were men. The man himself, at six foot three, deeply tanned and scarred, was a source of fascination to the women. Since the couple's arrival, business around the pool had picked up.

The pool was unusual: three circles, lined with blue tile of varying colors, met in the middle at a small island of volcanic rock and palm trees. Each circle was of different depth. Nile Barrabas and Erika Dykstra lay beside the deepest pool.

"What time is it?" Erika asked without moving.

"Four." Barrabas could see the clock over the pool attendant's booth from where he lay. "Time to go upstairs."

"For our usual? Let's go," Erika said with enthusiasm.

She rolled to a sitting position, reached for her bikini top and tied it, unaware of the audience she was attracting. With her long blond hair, startling green eyes and her magnificent body, she was stunning. Every man breathed a sigh as she stood and started toward the hotel veranda, her hips undulating in a slow jungle-sensuous rhythm. The wives and mothers breathed deeper sighs.

As they passed the porter's desk, Erika heard her name called. "An urgent message for you, *madame*," the hall porter said, handing her an envelope.

Erika Dykstra was an importer. Her family's ships had plied the seas for years out of their home port of Amsterdam. Now she was the head of the firm, Netherlands Imports Management, and she used air cargo to ensure that her goods reached their destinations in hours instead of days or weeks. Her brother Gunther, the only other surviving Dykstra, was content to let his sister run the show. He preferred to deal with people like Barrabas, running guns, selling or renting aircraft. His customers were mercs, people in a hurry to change history.

In their room, Erika stripped off her bikini and sat on the bed. She tore open the envelope and read the message hurriedly.

"I have to go soon," she said. "Trouble in Hong Kong with some Chinese artifacts we managed to export from the mainland."

"You mean 'smuggled,' don't you?" Barrabas smiled. He was more relaxed than he had been for weeks. But a week of fun in the sun was enough, even with Erika at his side. This was not the life for him. He had to have action.

Erika threw the message on a night table and stretched out on the bed. "Let's make the most of tonight. I'll have to go tomorrow."

Barrabas stripped and joined her on the bed. He ran his hand over the smooth skin of her thigh. Their lips met in a long, slow kiss.

The telephone rang. Erika laughed and rolled over, reaching for the receiver. Barrabas's smile disappeared, along with the urge building within him. He knew why the telephone had rung. He had a sixth sense about it.

Erika answered and then listened for a few seconds. "It's 'the Fixer,'" she said, holding out the receiver to him.

Walker Jessup, one of the fattest and shrewdest men in Washington, had been dubbed "the Fixer" by CIA colleagues.

"Nile, have you been catching the news?" he asked without any preliminaries. His voice left no doubt that he had something on his mind.

"No. We haven't seen a paper. No radio. What's up?"

"Congressman Weston was killed yesterday."

Barrabas sat beside Erika on the bed, speechless for a moment. Clint Weston had been a buddy in Nam. He hadn't seen Clint in over a year, but he'd followed his friend's progress in Congress. Weston had been one hell of a man.

"What happened?" he asked.

"You remember that the Soviets forced down a passenger liner in 1978?" Jessup asked. "Well, they shot one down yesterday. Two hundred and sixty-nine innocent people were killed. Mostly Koreans, but Weston was aboard."

Barrabas had nothing to say. He had seen hundreds of men killed in battle, men he'd admired, but this one hit home. He thought back to Vietnam and how he'd relied on Weston's judgment.

"I need you in Washington. Now," Jessup said.

Barrabas shook himself. "What's the play?" he asked.

"Get here as fast as you can. Call my office. I'll have all the information by then," he said. "We're going to need the team."

Barrabas put the phone down and sank to the bed beside Erika. The blond woman gazed at him, her blue eyes suddenly distant, masking her thoughts. Wordlessly she turned away to stare at the cerulean sky beyond the terrace window. Barrabas slipped his arm under her shoulder, pulling her close, feeling her pliant body nestle tentatively against his in a silent farewell.

WALKER JESSUP WASTED no time after his call to Barrabas.

He had to see the senator right away, the pint-size man of power whom the President went to when he wanted a "dirty" job done. Jessup waited until the vehicle came to a full stop in the basement garage of the Senate office building, then squeezed his bulk through the door and headed toward the elevator. The white limousine would be waiting in the same spot when he returned.

Jessup loved three things: money, action and food. He was known as the Fixer on Capitol Hill, and most of his money came from the little man who could look out across Maryland Street at the Supreme Court Building from his office on the top floor. Without him, Jessup wouldn't have had a seven figure unnumbered account in Bern, the penthouse in New York or the limo.

In his office, the senator was in no better mood than Jessup. He sat in the custom-made chair, looking out over the oversize desk, a Lilliputian dictator in his private domain.

"Are you a mind reader or just looking for more money?" he asked as Jessup took a seat before him. "You must be really salting it away."

"Nice to see you, too, Senator."

"I've just come from the White House. They're worried about the KAL thing. The Soviets claim we've been invading their airspace for years."

"Have we?" Jessup asked. As ex-CIA. he had few illusions.

"That's the hell of it. We can't be sure. The national security adviser is pointing the finger in every direction," the man said, leaning over and making his point by waving a bony finger in the fat man's face. "He thinks the CIA has been paying foreign pilots of commercial flights to overfly just to confuse the issue. Claims the Joint Chiefs are in league with the CIA and that we're sending in spy planes under the protection of civilian craft."

"That's got to be bullshit. Our spy satellites would pick that kind of thing up."

"Too bloody rational. This is Washington. There's a goddamned spy under every bush." The senator looked worried. "We've got to know, Jessup. We've got to know if it's the Soviets who are paranoid, or our own people. We need real proof. Something absolutely carved in stone."

"How about the Russians' computer files? That should do it."

"A hard probe into their own backyard. Barrabas and his soldiers?" the man asked.

The two men were a contrast in fat and thin. The senator's skin shone, stretched as it was, like polished parchment over bone. Jessup's bulk poured out around the chair, his multiple chins hiding what might have been the knot of an expensive tie.

"I don't know anyone else who could pull it off," Jessup said. "That goddamned place is a fortress. It's a suicide mission. This one's going to cost."

"We'll pay. One hundred thousand each. Tops."

"No way. Five hundred. You need a bloody army to go in there, and we're going in with less than ten."

"'We'? When the hell did you ever risk your ass?" the senator demanded. "All right. Five each, and you rake your commission off the top."

Jessup considered the offer for a brief moment. "It's a deal. I'll make sure the warriors get their share." Jessup knew he'd be on the wrong end of a SOB exercise, skewered like a steer ready for barbecue if they didn't.

"Now get the hell out, Jessup, and get those men on the way."

The Fixer pulled his massive three hundred pounds out of the chair, his mind on a plate of truffles for lunch and another pile of money for his account.

THE PARTING HAD BEEN SHORT. Barrabas and Erika had both withdrawn into silences, their feelings toward each other mixed with apprehension for the future. After dinner they had checked the airlines. Barrabas was able to get on a British Airways flight to Heathrow with a connection by Concorde to Washington. He would be in the capital for lunch the next day. Erika had decided to take a Singapore Airlines flight at nine-thirty the next day.

The flight to London was long and tiring. Barrabas, still relaxed from the week at Penang, slept most of the way. He had five hours at Heathrow to wait for the flight that would take him to Washington and to Walker Jessup.

He took a shuttle bus to a hotel and rented a room. He set his Rolex, a gift from Erika, for three hours later and lay back on the bed. His mind had been on Sakhalin and Clint Weston since Jessup's call. This one he was going to do for love and money. The guy had been a real friend.

The Sakhalin penetration would be tough. Though he hadn't met with Jessup, he could anticipate the mission. This was one time that he wished he had an army. His mind slipped away from the job and to the team.

Dr. Lee Hatton was at her place in Majorca, trying to put the ruined manor house back into shape after the Russian Balandin and his Spetsnaz had tried to eliminate the SOB team.

O'Toole, the irrepressible redheaded Irishman would be at Manny's Bar on the San Diego waterfront, drinking himself silly every night and reading his foul poetry when he wasn't sleeping in some fleabag hotel down the street.

William Starfoot II, the full-blooded Osage, had decided to spend some time with his oil-rich father in Oklahoma, trying to see if they could patch up some of their differences.

Claude Hayes and Alex "the Greek" Nanos, forever lovers of the briny, had bought a new Whitby 42 ketch-rigged sailboat at the Fort Myers shipyards, and had sailed her down the coast by way of the Dry Tortugas and the Keys, and up to Fort Lauderdale. They had filled her with beer and young beach bums of the female gender.

Nate Beck, the electronics wizard, had found a soul mate who could caress a computer as expertly as himself. He and the new friend, a multimillionaire escapee from Silicon Valley, were holed up in a Paris hotel room, cracking and compiling secret access codes for various international information systems. "Hey! They'll come in handy," Beck had told him with his fast-paced New York accent. In an era when electronic information was power, the Jewish genius was an important player.

Including Barrabas, that made seven. He could use a couple more hands but didn't have time to review Jessup's original files. They had lost a few along the way: Boone, Biondi, Chank Dayo and Emilio Lopez. He'd give his share of this operation for another Lopez. He missed the little son of a bitch. And then there was Geoff Bishop.

The whole team was still numb from the loss of the ace Canadian pilot. Geoff Bishop had bought it during the SOBs' mission to Florida, saving the life of the governor by giving his own. The sharks of Tampa Bay took what the bomb blast gave them—there hadn't even been a body. An easygoing ex-military man, Geoff was sorely missed. He had also been Lee Hatton's lover. The doctor had to tend to her own private grief. A new assignment would be good for her—it would get her mind off it.

Barrabas thought about the new job. How to get in was one problem. More important was how to get out. A small boat, and perhaps two inflatables would get them there. Then they would steal a plane to make their getaway fast. But with Geoff Bishop gone, he needed a pilot—pronto!

3

In a waterfront bar on India Street, just up from the *Star of India*'s berth, Liam O'Toole sat in a corner booth, with an overdeveloped frowsy blonde beside him. He was reading poems aloud from a loose-leaf binder, the culmination of his jumbled thoughts since his last job. In his right hand he guarded a full tumbler of Irish whiskey from marauding hands. A margarita glass, its dried salt scattered across the table, sat empty in front of the blonde. Her eyes were closed as she listened to the ramblings of the redheaded Irishman beside her. Her hand rested on his crotch, while part of her mind dwelled on the nights they'd spent in his dingy room a block away on Columbia.

The bartender loomed over them. "You're O'Toole, ain't you? Some guy from Washington calling," he said, picking up the woman's fluted glass and wiping the salt from the table onto the floor.

The big man squeezed out of the booth, sauntered uncertainly to the bar and picked up the ancient black phone.

"O'Toole," he said his speech slurred.

"Barrabas. Nanos and Hayes are in Lauderdale. Pick them up and meet me at Sumi Omatu's in

Tokyo,'' the voice of authority said. "Sober up Liam. And get there fast."

"I'm with you, Colonel. What about the others?" The voice was already rock-steady. When the battle loomed, the crazy Irishman was always ready.

"I'll call Hatton. She'll go direct from Majorca. Billy is in Oklahoma. I'll get him at his father's place. Nate is in Paris. I can pick them up on the way to Tokyo. We might need an extra body or two on this one. You got one we can use?" he asked. "You know what we need."

"Not offhand. You want me to look around?"

"No time. We'll have to go with what we've got. I'll see you in Tokyo."

ON THE SHORE of Lake Chickasha, north of Anadarko in Oklahoma Indian country, a huge mansion sat alone, surrounded by forest and stream. Relics of times past dotted the cluttered yard: a swaybacked teepee, rusting cooking pots, moth-eaten bear and buffalo skins. Old men sat on the wide wooden veranda that skirted three sides of the square red brick monolith. All but one were old. A huge man in war paint and breechcloth sat calmly among them, smoking the pipe and passing it along. A full-blooded Osage, a lot of history ran in his veins.

William Starfoot II sat at the feet of his father, the richest Oklahoma Indian oilman in history. It was a celebration. The son, Billy Two to his SOB friends, seldom came to the home of his father.

An old woman, her parched skin stretched tightly over high cheekbones, shambled from the house with a remote telephone in one hand, the antenna extended. She handed it to the young man without speaking.

"Billy? Nile Barrabas."

"Colonel." Billy Two was a man of few words.

"A job, Billy. I need you in Tokyo." Barrabas had known the American Indian for years. Starfoot was a former marine commando, an expert in survival techniques, martial arts, maps and charts.

"Omatu's?"

"Fast as you can."

"Do I have time for one night in the hills?" Billy asked.

Barrabas knew that the solitude of the hills was important to Billy Two. Once, the native American had been a victim of Spetsnaz, the elite Russian military intelligence agency. Injections of liquid sulfur had burned through his veins and into his consciousness, a gruesome torture that had changed him forever. He was still a one-man fighting machine, although at times difficult to control. He'd do anything to back up a fellow fighter. Barrabas was more concerned about Billy Two recklessly putting himself in the line of fire.

The stop in Paris might take a day. If Billy started the day after tomorrow, he would be in Tokyo soon enough.

"One night, Billy. Get your head straightened out and get on the plane."

IN A THREE-ROOM SUITE in the Hotel Dupliex in the *quinzième arrondissement* in Paris, almost in the shadow of the Eiffel Tower, Nate Beck sat before the console of a computer. Across the equipment-cluttered room, a young heavily-bearded man sat quietly, the green glow of a computer monitor changing his mouse-colored hair to a more sickly color.

The concierge and the maître d'hôtel had given up on them. The housekeeper wouldn't allow her women to enter the suite. Half-eaten meals cluttered every empty space. Beds were unmade. The room was beginning to smell like the city dump.

Barrabas knocked. When no one answered, he entered. The room was dark; all the blinds were pulled down. Only the green glow from a half-dozen monitors lit the room. It was a scene from the *Star Wars* command center or a local game arcade minus the noise.

He moved to Beck's console, placed an airline ticket folder on the keyboard under his "flying finger" and waited.

Beck picked up the folder and read the counterfoil. "Tokyo? Today?" he asked calmly.

"Get yourself cleaned up. I'll meet you at Orly in two hours. Our flight leaves in three."

O'TOOLE HAD TO USE all the persistence he had to get the show on the road. Nanos the Greek and Claude Hayes had taken on a partner, and the three of them had the salon on the Whitby 42 crammed with women. The females had two things in common, besides their sex. They were all naked, and they were all built like Marilyn Monroe.

The big red-haired Irishman had easily found the Lauderdale marina. The Whitby had been pointed out to him by a frazzled marina owner who loaned him a skiff. It was anchored, fore and aft, a hundred yards out, surrounded by a flotilla of smaller craft.

His friends were holding a Miss Nude Whitby 42 contest. O'Toole stood at the hatch and watched for a few minutes as the three men tried out their tape measures. Nanos and Hayes, he knew. The Greek and the black American had fought by his side often enough. The other man was a stranger.

He was Latin and totally bald, his polished pate reflecting light from the ports. He was short with a massive chest, potbelly and legs that looked no thicker than those of kitchen chairs. A tamped cigarillo was stored behind the ear with the gold earring.

O'Toole made his way down to the salon, put a hamlike hand on Nanos's shoulder and nodded for him to step outside. The white ketch-rigged boat was forty-two feet at the waterline, had a center cockpit, sported a red bimini and a white canvas sunshade over the fantail. Two deck chairs were open under the canvas.

"Who's your friend?" O'Toole asked when they were seated. No "Hello" and no "How you been?" They both knew what the visit meant.

"José Sanchez. Great guy."

"Where'd he come from?"

"You'll get a charge outa this. He's Stella Lopez's younger brother. Emilio's uncle. He looked up to him. The guy's unreal. At twenty, he forged papers saying he was a Mexican exchange officer for training at Bradbury Lines. He's been trained by the British Special Air Services, for chrissakes."

O'Toole was suspicious. "If he was an exchange officer, what happened when the British officer showed up over here?"

"Sanchez had forged orders cut for the deal both ways, used the name of a general in Mexico City, and no one had the guts to challenge it. Would you?" Nanos laughed, slapping O'Toole on the knee. He jumped up, scrambled down the hatch and came back with a half-dozen cans of beer.

"He finish the course at Bradbury Lines?" O'Toole asked. The British camp was the toughest air force training camp in the world.

"Yep."

"How old is he?"

"Early forties."

"He had to be in England the same time as Beckwith," O'Toole said with disbelief. The American Delta Force had had its origins there when Charlie Beckwith went there back in '62. This was beginning to sound like a tale told after too many whiskeys, a state he knew only too well. He took a swig of cold beer and waited.

"*With* Beckwith. Trained with the guy."

"No shit!" O'Toole was beginning to believe. "What's he done since?"

"You name it. Delta Force. A merc with 'Madman.' Commanded an Arab attack squadron in '67 and again in '73 against the Israelis. This guy's been there."

"Any chance of bullshit?"

"Nope. He called him one day. Charles Beckwith. In Washington. We all talked to him. Sounded like a great guy. Another day we're drifting around a couple of miles out, we drag out the weapons and call his bluff. He fieldstripped an M-16, my Uzi carbine and the M-60s we got stashed. Did it better and quicker than Hayes or I. Then, he showed us some real shooting. The guy's a real prize," the Greek concluded. "He's fun, too."

"Think he'd like to work?"

"He's been hanging around to get taken on. And I guess we need an airman now."

The squeals from below drifted up, and O'Toole could see Nanos squirming.

"Speak any language?" he asked.

"I tried him in Russian and German. He's a lot better than me. Says he speaks Arabic, some Hebrew. Why should he lie?"

"Sounds too good to be true. We're going to need him on this trip. He goes."

"All right! When?"

"Now. Yesterday. The colonel is already on the way."

"Where?"

"Omatu's in Tokyo. With the mess down below, I'd say you might make a plane out of Miami by noon tomorrow."

"You going to stay? There's plenty to go around." The Greek grinned, his white teeth a contrast to his heavy five o'clock shadow.

"See you in Tokyo," O'Toole declined. He tossed back his beer and headed for the dock.

THE EASIEST FLIGHT OUT of Majorca for Lee Hatton
was with Scandinavian Airlines through Copenhagen. She had had a great deal of her father's home re-
built during her stay on the island. The original
building had been demolished by Captain Balandin of
the GRU, Russian Military Intelligence, in an attempt
to eliminate the SOBs. The self-important captain had
once tried to rape her. She had caused him permanent
injury during the attempt. The man had never for-
given her.

For a long time Lee had left Majorca, choosing to
spend the weeks or months between assignments else-
where. As a medical doctor, she had volunteered to
work for various health agencies in Africa, joking to
the other mercs that it made up for her dark days with
some of Washington's more secretive—and nefar-
ious—intelligence agencies.

Much of her time had also been spent with Geoff
Bishop, at his lodge on a lake north of Montreal. Their
affair had been a kind of "open secret" among the
other mercs—on hold the moment a mission began.
Then the worst had happened. Bishop was dead. She
wasn't bitter. They all took risks and assumed the
consequences. But the airman's absence left an ach-
ing emptiness in her life.

Whatever the new job was, she was looking forward to it. It would take her mind off her loss. An
irony, she thought, that war can heal.

At Copenhagen's Kastrup airport, Dr. Hatton
bought a copy of *The Times*, which reported the full
list of dead and missing from the KAL flight. Nine
Canadians had been aboard. She recognized a name.

George Eastman had been an old friend of Geoff's, and she had met him on several occasions.

Bishop and Eastman had grown up together on the Manitoba prairies. They had learned to fly at the same time and had flown the Canadian North from Labrador to James Bay in their twenties.

As the flight droned on through the night, her thoughts returned again and again to the KAL flight. *The Times* reported that it had gone down in La Pérouse Strait between Hokkaido and Sakhalin islands. Japan wasn't that far from the crash site. Maybe she would have time to do some private investigation. It would depend on what the colonel had lined up for them.

The DC-10 approached Narita airport at Tokyo. Whatever the assignment was, Lee resolved to stay behind when it was over and find out more about the KAL disaster. For Geoff. For old time's sake.

4

The old house on Hibiya Dori Street creaked under the gusts of wind blowing in from Tokyo Bay. Nile Barrabas sipped from a small porcelain cup of hot sake. A servant had brought the pot of steaming firewater to him. In his halting Japanese, he explained she should not return until called for, then he turned his full attention to the friends gathered in the small second-floor room.

It was no more than twenty feet square, walled with the usual Japanese rice paper in muted floral patterns. A small rock garden occupied one corner. It was a place to meditate—a retreat. The table in the center was low, but had a shallow space below for those who could not squat in the Oriental fashion.

Everyone had made their way to Tokyo and had arrived within a twenty-four-hour period. Two faces were unfamiliar to some members of the group. Both newcomers were totally bald, and Barrabas thought they resembled squatting Buddhas. One sported a Pancho Villa mustache and had round eyes. The other had the long, sparse beard of an Oriental. His eyes were slanted. Neither man displayed any emotion.

Barrabas indicated the man on his right. "This is Sumi Omatu, our host. Most of you have met him," he said. "He will gouge every dollar he can from us, but his products are first class." He hesitated, looking around the group. "Liam will work with him on plastics. We need as much C-4 as two men can carry. Should have at least three dozen blasting caps and timers. O'Toole and Hayes will carry it in.

"Billy will select our firepower," he continued. "We'll each carry a small automatic weapon, maybe an Armalite or an Uzi carbine. The trick is to go in light, but to carry as much ammo as possible. If we need more powerful weapons later, we'll have to steal them."

Everyone listened carefully, sipped their hot sake or warm beer. Their eyes shifted from Sumi to the other bald man. This one would be going in with them, would be holding a weapon, perhaps protecting their asses. They would need to know about him.

"This is José Sanchez. He'll take over for Geoff as our team airman on this mission," Barrabas continued. "He's been working with Alex and Claude in Florida."

"That's hardly a recommendation, unless this is an exercise in rape and pillage," Lee joked bravely in the face of her lover's replacement.

"Only two items you need to know," Barrabas went on. "José graduated from Bradbury Lines in '63 with Charlie Beckwith and has fought his own wars around the world since then. He's Emilio's uncle, Stella's younger brother."

At the mention of Emilio, they sat silent for a moment. Then, Billy Two held out a hand across the table. José grasped it. The others reached out, placed a hand on the clasped fists, one by one, until they formed a pyramid of knuckled flesh. Lee Hatton's was on top. Omatu sat nearby, a silent impassive Buddha, as their witness.

They were silent for a moment, each with private thoughts. The names of Emilio Lopez and Geoff Bishop held a reminder of their own mortality. They didn't need to think about that part of it. The dying.

As usual, Dr. Hatton was the first to ask the obvious. Lee was a dark-haired beauty, and a match for any man in a firefight. "You wouldn't tell us on the phone. What's so important?"

"You've read or heard about the KAL flight downed by the Soviets near here," Barrabas stated, assuming assent. "The Russians are getting some bad press. Their propaganda defense includes an attempt to involve our government. They have accused our people of overflying the Russian fortified islands along the coast." He looked from one to the other. "The people in Washington don't have the answer. Why do commercial jets stray off course when they have fail-safe navigation systems to warn them? Why do they fly on when challenged?" He stopped for a few seconds to take a swallow of sake, letting the fire of it spread to his gut.

The six-foot-six Billy Two sat, cross-legged in the fashion of his people, a hot cup of sake untouched in front of him. "You think some hawks in the Pentagon have something going, Colonel?"

"We've been asked to find out. Five hundred thousand each minus the Fixer's fifteen percent, a third deposited to your accounts today."

"So what are we talking about?" Liam O'Toole asked. "Shit! We're fighting men." He waved an arm around the room at all of them, including Lee Hatton. "What the hell's this got to do with us? We're not intelligence types."

Barrabas was patient with his people. Liam had been an army captain, first class as a leader in battle, but he was not a politician and never would be.

"No agent could get what we need," he said. "We've got to go in and take it by force. We have an agent inside the KGB, but he can't get to it."

"What's so goddamned important about the Russian thing? Why us?" Claude Hayes asked. The big black man, a specialist in African politics and languages as well as in underwater demolition, had been in the middle of the "wars of liberation" on the dark continent until it sickened him. He had lived at the Majorca place with Lee for months before the Spetsnaz raid had ruined it. He'd fought at her side when the Spetsnaz attacked, and he'd helped to restore her father's dream. They were close, and he'd given Lee a shoulder to lean on when Geoff Bishop died. Now he hung out with Alex Nanos, the mad Greek. They were both frogmen and could sail anything that floated.

The room was silent for a full minute. A slight breeze moved the paper walls, sounding like dried leaves against a shingled roof. It was hot. Sweat glands were overworked, competing with the smell of hot sake and warm beer.

Nate Beck raised bright eyes to his chief, a smile spreading across his face. "They've got to have it on computer somewhere. If I could get at their computer banks—maybe by modem, or bring out a magnetic tape..." He was thinking out loud and hitting bull's-eyes.

Again the room was silent. "Any questions?" Barrabas asked. "Or should I just spell it out for you?"

No one spoke. They all concentrated on the colonel, waiting for his next words. "Nate hit it on the head," he said. "Sakhalin Island is the key. The Russians have made it the toughest fortress on their eastern flank." He hesitated for a few seconds, looking at each face in turn, the faces of the warriors he'd fought alongside. "Our agent will meet us, take us to a safehouse and provide maps. We have to find the computer storage building, breech it, come out with the answers.

"The whole place is full of foreign ships trying to find the black box," he went on. "Everyone is buzzing around there at once.

"That helps us," Barrabas said. "All the ships are in the strait between Hokkaido and Sakhalin. La Pérouse Strait. We'll be picked up at Wakkanai docks at 0300 tomorrow. We will be supplied with inflatables and dropped off at our target area. With all the excitement in the strait, we should be able to move around without creating suspicion."

"Why not fly in?" José Sanchez asked. "What's my job if we're going in by boat?"

"Can't. The island is alive with radar. They have hundreds of fighters based there, their new Foxhounds. I'm hoping we can steal something for you to fly us out.''

"So we go in by boat," O'Toole said. "But this could be a trap."

For a few seconds no one in the room had anything to say. Lee Hatton finally broke the silence. "This isn't going to be easy—going into the Russians' most heavily fortified island and coming out with state secrets. Why is Jessup so sure we need this?" she asked.

"The President, the national security adviser, the secretary of state—they all smell something rotten in this. They think someone is trying to shaft us, and it could be coming from the inside," Barrabas said. "They've got to be sure."

"Okay," Nanos said. "How do we get in? What can we carry?"

"First, as Liam points out, it could be a trap. We have enemies who will probably expect us to be sent in. Second, we have transport and cover provided by our navy salvage fleet, thanks to Jessup. We have to limit ourselves to the light automatic weapons Billy will pick out. We should have body armor, carry Berettas and some fragmentation grenades. Nate and Liam will both carry in explosives, as we said. Lee will carry in a supply of Pentothal and scopolamine. We may have to drag some information from somebody." He stopped and poured another cup of hot sake.

"Beck could be the key man on this one. The computer center is our objective. They want us to bring back a tape, or send back info by modem if we can find the lines to get it out. So Nate has to find what he needs here, maybe from Sumi, and pack it in with us.

Nanos will carry a supply of gas canisters and provide respirators for everyone. He and O'Toole speak Russian. If necessary, they will pose as locals or Soviet military."

He turned to Sanchez. "I understand you speak Russian."

"Enough to pose as a sentry."

"Good enough. I've got a job for you before that. We need night black fatigues for the team; webbing, boots. You know what we'll need. Okay. That's it. If we run short or need some heavy firepower, we may be able to break into an arms depot once we're inside." Barrabas stopped speaking for a few seconds and looked at the faces around the table. "Jessup says our agent has a safehouse set up for us. Let's hope it is safe."

"How the hell safe could it be?" Nanos asked. "If it's a setup, we'll walk right into it."

"I never told you it would be easy." Barrabas grinned, downing the sake in one gulp.

"Sometimes I wonder if it's worth the money, you know?" Hayes spoke for the first time. "I know we all need the action, the high. Sure, it's that, too. But in Africa, I had a personal stake in the mission—something that could get the juices flowing." He paused and looked around the table. "This one seems like a mechanical operation—no real cause, you know?"

Barrabas hadn't intended to bare his soul and didn't like locker-room speeches, but this seemed like a good time. "A United States congressman was killed when the U-15 blasted the Korean flight. Congressman Clint Weston was a Nam vet, one hell of a guy. He cared

about people. Weston helped me out of a bad spot
when he should have been worried about his own ass,"
he said, looking around the group.

No one spoke for a moment. It was always the same
before battle. They knew someone might not come
back. They might all be victims of Sakhalin's strength.
But they would go.

Lee broke the silence. "Something else you should
know. A friend of Geoff's was on that jet. He didn't
pull Geoff out of a firefight, but they had been close—
they learned to fly together, into the northern bush
and through some tricky spots. You don't find too
many friends like that. His name was George Eastman. He didn't deserve to die from a Russian heat-
seeking missile."

They were seven men and one woman with eight
different reasons for being there. Mutual respect—as
warriors and as friends—bound them to each other.

"All right," Barrabas broke the silence. "You all
have work to do. The Navy will have a helicopter
waiting for us at the airport at 0200 hours tomorrow.
We change in the helicopter and get to the docks by
three. Omatu's people will show you the supplies. Pick
out what we need. Meet here at 0100 hours, and Sumi
will lead you to me at the airport. That's it."

MIDNIGHT. The sky was as black as soot and almost
as thick. Captain Jonas Frost stood on the bridge of
the USS *Potomac*, cursing the wind, the sky and every
ship within twenty miles. He wished he'd never heard
of La Pérouse Strait or the Undersea Recovery Group.
Even the Merchant Marine looked good to him now.

"I'm going to the wardroom," he called out to the duty officer as he got out of his swivel chair and headed below.

As he walked down the passageway out of the wind, Frost started to take off his foul-weather gear. He hung his oilskins on a hook behind the wardroom door and headed for the coffee urn. A yeoman steward poured for him and then handed him a steaming mug.

Commander Tony Gray, his number one, sat at a table with his shoulders hunched, a two day's growth of beard challenging regulations by its presence. Frost's own face had gone even longer without a razor. For five days, the two men had moved from bridge to wardroom to their bunks—had probably averaged four hours of sleep out of twenty-four.

"How's it going, Skipper?" Gray asked.

"Not good. We have two submersibles down, two in for repairs. It's a bloody war down there. Our guys spend more time fighting off foreign divers than scanning the bottom. I've seen less combat during a beachhead assault."

"Have you found out what's so goddamned important that we've lost four men?"

"A congressman went down with the plane. Briefcase full of classified material, which could mean 'eyes only' to 'damned interesting.' The admiral didn't say. Probably doesn't know any more than we do."

"Damn! This is about as bad as it gets short of all-out war," Gray said.

"Not quite." Frost raised his bloodshot eyes to look at his friend. They had sailed tin cans together as far back as Korea, had transferred to URG at the same time. "Got this message while you were sacked out. Got a job for you."

"Let me guess. I've got to break off duty to rescue a two-master filled with ugly old women."

"Something like that. Seems we may have a team of spooks on our hands. You're to take a tender to the docks at Wakkanai and bring them out here. We're to break off, move in close to Mys Aniva, supply them with two inflatables and give them a bearing."

"Shit! Are you serious?" Gray asked, wiping a hand across his forehead. His eyes showed the fatigue of five days' work with little sleep and no success. "Break off after what we've been through, then try to resume position in this pack of sharks? As soon as we pull out, they'll be fighting for this spot. Is this why we busted our asses to get here first? Shit!"

"Yours is not to reason why, buddy." Frost grinned. "Might be a welcome diversion. Look, we do the best we can, right? We take orders and ferry spooks where they want to go. We dive and we recover." Frost filled an old briar with a Dutch blend and lit it. "You've been in this man's Navy long enough to know better than to fight it. Go with the flow. If you fight it, you're in trouble."

"Why can't I just take them direct to Mys Aniva by tender? I could take the inflatables. No sweat, and we wouldn't lose our position here."

"Because they can be launched easier from this ship. Besides, it's all spelled out in the orders. You've heard of orders," Frost answered, still grinning and puffing on his pipe as the overhead vents hungrily sucked at the smoke.

Gray looked at his skipper and wondered how the man stayed so calm. But he was right. He had to stop fighting it. Take orders. Pass them along. Get the job done. Maybe the spooks would give him a few hours' diversion. Who knows?

"Best get with it, Commander. You've got to be at the docks by 0300."

"Isn't this a job for one of the junior officers?" Gray asked. It was not an unreasonable question.

"Believe it or not, someone up there likes you. Your name was specified in the orders."

The exhausted commander pulled himself erect, gulped down the last of his coffee and, rolling with the ship, slipped out of the wardroom.

5

The truck transporting most of the SOBs pulled up to a Falcon 50 executive jet with USAF markings and full camouflage. Barrabas stood at the ramp, ushered everyone aboard, and then closed the hatch before going forward to talk to the pilot. They were taxiing for takeoff within seconds.

"Thought you said a chopper, Colonel," Nanos said.

"Too slow. Wakkanai is almost five hundred miles. A chopper will meet us at the airport and take us to the docks."

"Plush," Lee said.

"Belongs to the commanding general, Pacific Command," Barrabas said without elaboration.

The seats had been removed and replaced with a dozen swivel chairs that formed a full circle. The SOBs dumped their bags on the floor at their feet and prepared for takeoff.

"Once we're airborne, I want everyone in full gear." Barrabas turned to William Starfoot II. "Let's see what you've got, Billy," he said.

Billy Two opened one of the huge rucksacks he'd carried on board. He pulled out a submachine gun wrapped in oiled paper. "I couldn't get Uzis, Colonel. Omatu had a case of the new Italian Socimi 821s," he said, unwrapping the small gun. "It weighs only two and a half kilograms, fires 9 mm ammo. The clip holds thirty-two rounds. Six hundred rounds a minute on full auto. It's accurate to a hundred yards on single shot."

"We've never used the Socimi, Billy," Barrabas said. "Is it reliable?"

"I test-fired one, Colonel. Easy control with one hand. Changing the magazine is a snap," Billy said.

Sanchez spoke up. "I've used them, Colonel. Very reliable," he said. "Ammo's compatible with the Beretta 93-R. I'd say he made a good choice."

"What did you come up with, Sanchez?" Barrabas asked.

"Black turtlenecks, night black fatigues, para-trooper boots," he said. "Omatu had a gun shop in one of his warehouses. I was able to make special harnesses for this show. They'll take the Berettas, a commando knife, six HE grenades and each has a shoulder pouch. Lee can use it for her drugs. The rest of us can use it for the MU-50-G grenades I found."

"So we're going in with Italian hardware," Barrabas said. "Could be worse. I've used the grenades. Small but effective. How many to a man?"

"Sixteen each," Sanchez replied. "I brought a dozen black toques, if anyone wants one. They'll see your white hair a mile away, Colonel."

"That's it?" Barrabas asked, impressed with his new man.

"No, Colonel. A dozen Kevlar vests. The new ones with flaps that cover the ass and thighs. The toques have Kevlar skullcaps. They won't take much of a hit, but it might mean the difference."

"Thanks, Sanchez. Okay. Sounds like we have everything. When the plane levels off, full battle dress. We'll use the toques and black face," Barrabas said. "The forecast is for low cloud cover for the next twenty-four hours."

By the time he'd finished, his people were standing and shedding their street clothes. Sanchez was the only one who glanced in Lee's direction. By the time they slipped their Berettas into holsters and snapped on grenades, the plane was beginning its descent into Wakkanai.

"What's in the bag, Billy?" Barrabas asked.

"I know you said no heavy artillery, Colonel. But I just couldn't pass it up." He opened the sack and pulled out an Mk-19 grenade launcher.

"I know that brute could save our ass, Billy, but we're going to be in some cramped spots. The damned thing is heavy. It's designed to be mounted on something," Barrabas said. "Where the hell are you going to put it?"

"No mount, Colonel. I'll hold it," the big Indian said, grinning through the black grease on his face.

"Your problem," Barrabas said. He turned to the others. "From here to the beach we maintain silence. The Navy knows where we're going. If they have to talk, they'll talk to me."

TONY GRAY YAWNED and turned red-rimmed eyes toward the helipad again. They were fifteen minutes late. If they had to hit the beach before dawn, they'd have to hurry. He opened the hatch and went on deck, stood by his helmsman and lit a cigarette. It was dark. He wouldn't see the chopper until it was almost on top of them.

Then he heard it. Within seconds, the chopper circled in, set down and discharged its cargo. Eight black figures ran in single file toward the boat. They came aboard, climbed down the ladder and entered the chart room without saying a word. Gray ordered the boat to cast off, and at a full forty-five knots, they churned the waters of the strait toward the mother ship.

Gray was very curious about the group. Eight figures of varying heights, all in black. They all carried small automatic weapons and holstered hand guns. He noted the commando knives, the gas masks and the HE grenades. The tallest man carried what looked like a 40 mm machine gun. He hadn't seen a group like that since he'd toured the Navy commando school. But these commandos were different. The school had been for practice. This was for real. He had never seen a group like this—not quite like this. Despite his years in the service, he shuddered.

When they were halfway to the ship, Commander Gray went below. The eight were sitting in a circle. They looked up at him dispassionately, faces streaked with black. A tuft of white hair showed beneath one toque, a strand of red beneath another. Sixteen eyes stared into his—cold eyes, eyes of all colors. Their mouths were compressed. Their faces were calm, un-smiling.

He was about to speak but decided he had nothing of any importance to say. He turned and climbed the hatch ladder to wait for their arrival.

When the tender pulled alongside the mother ship, Gray led the way up from the landing grid to the deck. Sensing that the SOBs had no intention of going through any formalities, he led them belowdecks to the launchpad. They were in the stern of the ship at about the waterline. Hinged ten-foot square steel doors were guarded by two seamen.

Two inflatables sat on the gray steel deck, their bows pointed out to sea. Twenty-five horsepower Johnsons were attached to the aft thwarts, tipped at an angle, their props six inches from the deck. Each boat would take six men, and each would easily cruise at ten knots with enough fuel for about four hours. They would be abandoned at the beachhead.

Gray left the group to examine the inflatables and made his way to the bridge. Captain Frost was peering out across the strait.

"Are your charges aboard, Commander?" Frost asked.

"Yes, sir," Gray replied.

"Up anchor," he commanded.

"Up anchor," Gray passed along.

"Set course for two seven five degrees," Frost commanded.

"Two seven five degrees, sir," the helmsman responded.

"Give me all the knots we have," Frost said to Gray, who relayed the command below.

"You're quiet, Commander. Something wrong?" Frost asked.

"They're not real, Captain. I've seen commandos before, but never anything like that crew. Not regulation, either. They all have foreign weapons. I'm almost sure one is a woman."

"Which just proves you're not getting enough sleep. After they're launched, I suggest you take an extra hour in your bunk."

Gray was silent for a minute or two. Frost turned his attention to checking on their course and the ETA.

"It's not the sleep, Captain. It's them. You've got to see them to understand."

"Did they talk to you?" Frost asked.

"Not a goddamned word."

"Then they won't greet me with open arms. Let's get them to where they're going and then forget about them."

Gray's thoughts turned inward. You may forget about them, Captain. But they'll haunt my dreams. He thought about Sakhalin, about what it must be like. A frigging fortress. Maybe they were a match for Sakhalin. Maybe the Soviets deserved the team.

IT WAS ALMOST DAWN when they went in. La Pérouse Strait was swelled by an inshore chop. Westerlies blew a cold wind in from a churning sea. Black clouds rolled in, low and menacing, the remnants of a typhoon burning itself out in the Pacific.

The fleet of salvage vessels rolled in the mid-strait swells. The SOBs' delivery vessel was almost back in the mass of retrieval ships, a speck on the horizon. The mercs had seen the chaos in the middle of the strait: spotlights ablaze, megaphones held to angry mouths shouting obscenities from one ship to another. It wasn't the floor of the United Nations. It was the real world of blood and sweat. The ships of five nations fought to be the one to bring up the black box or something else that might indicate what had happened. Deep beneath the cold black water, men dived to find this treasure.

Hatton and Hayes helped Barrabas load their dinghy before pushing off. O'Toole, Nanos, Beck, Sanchez and Billy Two followed within twenty feet. Hayes and Nanos, the seamen, took command.

The sea was rough, the night black. Even at twenty feet, they had trouble seeing the silhouettes in the other boat. They were to rendezvous at Mys Aniva, a peninsula at the southern tip of the island. The signal was to be one short and two long.

Barrabas didn't like the whole setup; there had not been enough planning. The contact on Sakhalin was too tenuous. They had no backup, insufficient firepower and didn't speak the language. If the information that brought them in was false, it was unlikely that they would get out alive.

Soon the group could hear a roar of surf ahead. In the lead boat, Hayes squinted through the darkness and picked up a white froth. If it was a reef, their rubber boats would be torn to shreds on the sharp coral shards. The charts had shown no reefs, but Hayes did not want to take any chances.

Finally Hayes saw a gap in the foam. He headed in and surfed toward shore on a huge wave that followed. He hoped Nanos, commanding the dinghy behind, had the same luck.

As they approached shore, the darkness grew even thicker. They could see white froth on the shore and something else. As they grew closer, Barrabas made out the shape of a cross—a crucifixion.

The lead dinghy rushed through shifting sand and came to rest five feet from the water's edge. Nanos and his passengers drifted in behind.

The eight SOBs pulled their craft ashore and then turned them around, facing the boiling surf. They spread out, their Socimis unslung from their shoulders. Gradually they converged on the cross, which was two sun-bleached tree limbs lashed together.

The moon peeked out from a cloud for a few seconds, illuminating a grotesque white face. A man had been crucified. Naked, blood running from his battered torso, he was still breathing, barely, his face a mask of pain. A crude sign hung from his neck.

Greetings! Your man Moltsov awaits anxiously. Let us hope your stay on Sakhalin will be a happy one.

Colonel Yuri Popolov

Moltsov opened his pain-racked eyes briefly. From lips crusted with blood, he muttered a word of warning. Then he died.

As the mercs prepared to ease him down from the cross, AK-47s opened up from nearby dunes. Slugs tore the body to shreds and sprayed the SOBs with blood. A dozen searchlights split the darkness, probing for the black figures on the beach.

Covered with blood and brain matter from the shredded spy, the SOBs dug into the soft sand as bullets pierced the killing ground around them. Their silenced Socimis coughed single rounds as they tried to pick off selective targets—the searchlights, anything.

Suddenly, behind them, the roar of the Mk-19 drowned out the sound of enemy fire. The big 40 mm launcher could spit out grenades at 375 rounds a minute, but the giant arms holding the bucking machine gave it short bursts, five or six at a time, blackening spotlights, shredding bodies.

Billy Two stopped firing. The wind carried the noise of screams and curses. An offshore breeze carried the smell of cordite and blood inland. The wash of waves on the shore was the only sound they could hear.

''Liam. Take them back to the boats. Wait for us at ankle depth,'' Barrabas shouted.

The AK-47s opened up again, their fire not as concentrated. No SOBs had been hit, but they had to get the hell out of there. A grenade landed forty feet in front of them, forcing them to the ground. Billy Two spotted the flash and fired a dozen 40 mms at the spot. He held down the trigger and sprayed the whole area with the small but effective grenades until the last of the disintegrating link belt of his ammo ran out. The can was filled with nothing but empty cases. He threw the Mk-19 on the sand and unslung his Socimi.

The inflatables were in the water. Barrabas gave cover fire, but the targets were elusive. He and Billy turned for the boats, waded up to their knees and threw themselves over the plastic gunwhales.

Two wounded Soviets dragged themselves to the beach and fired sporadically. The native American was hit in the right buttock as he tried to pull himself aboard. Two slugs tore into the boat.

Hatton stood in the undamaged boat. With her Socimi on single shot, she put two slugs into each of the Russian survivors.

"Nanos!" Barrabas called from the sinking boat. "We're coming aboard. Get us the hell out of here!"

With all eight SOBs on board, the overloaded inflatable crossed the choppy water of Aniva Bay just as the light of dawn started to make a new horizon. It was starting to rain, lightly at first, then in drops that cut visibility to almost zero.

Lee Hatton had examined Billy's wound and found that the Kevlar flap had saved him a lot of pain. He had one hell of a bruise, and he'd sit carefully for a few days, but the skin hadn't even been broken. Billy Two knew who had saved his ass and nodded to Sanchez. The veteran warrior nodded back. A bond was beginning to take root.

"Take us in close," Barrabas called to Nanos. "If you see any buildings up the coast, we'll slip in for a look."

"I can see one now, Colonel," Nanos replied.

"Where do you put us right now?"

"We rounded the point at Mys Krilon a mile back, Colonel. I can't see worth a damn, but I'm sure I saw a building on that headland ahead."

"You're the sailor. How are we doing?" Barrabas asked. He didn't like the sound of something as exposed as a building on a headland.

"I don't like it, Colonel. The storm is getting worse. We're overloaded and running short on fuel."

"Right," Barrabas called over the wind. "Let's do it. Head in."

Nanos turned to run with the swells into shore. There was no beach along that part of the coast. They were lucky it was the lee side of the island, but it was rocky, and Nanos knew they might have to sink the boat and wade ashore. As they came within twenty yards, he knew for sure.

"Only one chance, Colonel. We can't run in here and come out again. Got to scuttle her and make sure she can't be spotted from the air," Nanos shouted over the wind, which was picking up by the minute.

Barrabas nodded and pointed to the land. Everyone had heard. When they were ten yards out, they dived over the side and headed for the rocky shore. Nanos and Hayes slit the boat with commando knives and threw the motor over the sinking hull. She went down in ten feet of murky water.

Waves bashed against the rocks, but every member of the team managed to grab an outcropping and pull himself up without injury. They crawled up the side of the headland, half expecting a welcoming committee. If they had left survivors on the beach, the whole south end of the island would be alerted. Even if they had killed every man in the firefight, some of the enemy might have been in communication with their headquarters.

The SOBs were soaked to the skin. Their weapons had been exposed to saltwater. They had no assurance that the house on the headland would be of any use, or if any other building would be available for miles.

Rain poured out of a black and ugly sky.

6

The house sat on the headland, a solitary sentinel daring the elements to attack it. The SOBs crawled from the cliff's edge and fanned out in their approach of the building. They expected an attack at any moment.

O'Toole frog-walked to the back door through the muck of a barnyard. The door opened to his hand. Sanchez slid past him, a phantom in search of the enemy. The house appeared to have been empty for some time.

The others followed, their mud-caked feet tracking into the kitchen and through the halls. There was very little furniture in the house. In the upstairs bedrooms two old dressers produced worn sheets that were being used by mice as nesting grounds. In the shed at the rear, they found a pile of hardwood. A massive pot-bellied stove sat in one corner of what was probably the living room.

"What you think, Colonel?" O'Toole asked. "We got anything to lose by lighting a fire?"

"Not in this downpour. Let's see if it works," he said. "But not you, Liam. If you want dry clothes, you'll have to fight someone for them. I want to see you, Nanos and Sanchez in the kitchen, now. Let Billy light the fire.''

In the kitchen Barrabas sat on his haunches, pulled off his wet toque and turned to the others as they came in. "We need Russian uniforms, heavier weapons and transport. You three are nominated. Leave your weapons here, take only your knives. Bring back what we need, including some food.''

The three were veterans; they needed no further instructions. While they were gone, the others would clean the weapons and ammo they had, dry their clothes, prepare for an exit to another safehouse.

"One last thing,'' Barrabas said. "When you take out the Russians, we don't want their bodies to show up. I understand the Soviet army is being plagued with desertions. Alcoholism is rampant. If they cannot be found, they'll be assumed deserters. Try for foot soldiers; they're more likely to desert than officers.

"Do you have the identification papers Sumi put together?'' he asked.

The three men unzipped their chest pockets and produced waterproof pouches with the false ID. They gave their leader only a parting glance as they moved to the back door and out into the rain.

The three men split up at the bottom of the long, rutted road that intersected with one running north and south. Sanchez took the south road to the coast, hoping to find a lone sentry post.

O'Toole and Nanos struck out to the north. An hour later, at about eight in the morning, they came to a fork in the road, one leading along the coast, the other heading inland. Without comment, Nanos started up the coast road.

O'Toole headed inland. It was a strange feeling to be all alone heading into the center of an unknown island, an island as heavily fortified as any in the world. Barrabas knew what they were up against, but it was clear their leader had decided to go through with the job. If he'd decided to pull out, he'd have sent them to find a boat.

His boots were soon soggy and made squishing noises with each step. The wool socks he'd put on had bunched and gathered. Each step was torture.

A light glowed through the downpour, illuminating a shack that was perched on the side of the road.

O'Toole crept up as quietly as he could considering the noise his boots made. The downpour muffled the sound. Through a dusty window he saw a soldier studying a book. It looked like the Russian version of *Penthouse*—obviously black market.

The shack was about eight feet by eight. The soldier had his greatcoat off and was sitting with his feet up on a small stove.

O'Toole picked up a rock the size of a cantaloupe and eased open the door.

It screeched on dry hinges.

The Russian acted instinctively as the big Irishman raised the rock. He jumped to his feet, ducked and then punched O'Toole in the mouth.

The two men went down, locked in mortal combat.

AT THE FARMHOUSE, the stove roared. Clothes were strung out on lines made from old lamp cords. Steam rose from the wet clothes to mist the dust-covered windows. Rivers of condensation ran down the panes, carrying dirt to form small puddles on the sills.

By nine, most of the weapons had been soaked in rain water to get rid of the salt and were then stripped and dried. Billy Two had brought a small can of machine oil that they used sparingly.

By ten, Barrabas was satisfied that the weapons would be usable, but he was beginning to worry about his scouts. Without a vehicle and another place to stay, closer to their target, they might as well find a boat and get the hell out.

But he wasn't about to abort the mission. Beck's equipment had been sealed in plastic and was still usable. They had their weapons. Their clothes would soon be dry. He waited anxiously for his scouts to return with a vehicle—and some food.

SANCHEZ COULDN'T REMEMBER the last time he'd been so wet and so alone. He kept thinking about the five hundred thousand. He'd knocked around the world, and he'd been in worse spots than this. But he'd never been paid this much. Any sacrifice was worth that kind of money.

He trudged on for a mile until the road turned inland. He didn't see a house, an animal or a human. It made sense. Why would anyone want to live in this area?

Another mile, then another. Finally, just as he was beginning to give up hope, the road came to an abrupt end. With the heavy rain, he couldn't see more than a few feet.

There was nothing between him and the deserted farmhouse. He hoped O'Toole or Nanos had had better luck and he turned back.

ALEX NANOS WAS a born scrounger. Every unit needed one. The weather didn't bother him. He'd been a sailor too long to let a little water get to him. It was his gut that was bothering him. He hadn't eaten for hours, and that was not his style. A full belly and a full bed. That was Alex Nanos.

He had walked about three miles after leaving O'Toole before he saw the farmhouse. He crept to the kitchen window. A peasant sat with his wife at the kitchen table, viewing slides through an old-fashioned eyepiece. He hadn't seen one of those for thirty years, not since an old aunt had shown him some pictures of his relatives. Though the morning light was almost full, an oil lamp burned brightly on the table in front of them. A long-haired dog was curled up by the kitchen stove, oblivious to the intruder not fifteen feet away.

Nanos scouted the barn. He found chickens, smoked hams and fresh eggs. In a cold cellar under the floor, he found a cache of black bread. But he had to know more about the road. He hadn't found any military personnel, and that was his first priority. He picked up one of the big white eggs, punched a hole in one end and sucked out the contents.

Nanos trudged down the farmhouse road and headed north again. In about a mile, the road ended at the ruins of an old barn. He headed back to the farm, found an old cloth sack and half filled it with food. The chickens squawked, but that couldn't be heard from the house. He took one in each hand and swung them until their necks broke. He took four chickens, one ham, two dozen eggs and three loaves of bread. He didn't worry about footprints. The barn floor was covered in old straw, and the rain persisted outside.

O'TOOLE CAME TO HIS SENSES with one hell of a headache. A young face stared at him, eyes filled with curiosity but not life. The fist that had almost crushed O'Toole's jaw had spent many hours at hard labor, but the rock that caved in its owner's skull was harder.

The big Irishman grasped a chair unsteadily and pulled himself up, wavering for a few minutes before looking for a lifeline. He found it in the bottom drawer of a beaten-up old desk. A small flask of white liquid. If he was lucky, it would be vodka.

It was vodka, fiery vodka. He raised the flask to his lips, threw back his head. Then he stopped.

One of the Colonel's strictest rules was no drinking on the job. It was a rule he'd never broken—and Liam O'Toole had survived worst fixes without it. He looked at the lovely liquid with regret, tipped the bottle and watched it pour on the floor.

He reached for the young soldier, pulled off his coat and tried it on. The fit was perfect. He had just finished exchanging his clothes when he heard the noise of an engine.

Shit! He grabbed the dead man's Kalashnikov. It was clean and well cared for. He released the safety, stroked the cocking lever and set it for single shot. He was not a wasteful man.

The vehicle pulled up outside.

Keeping the peak of his cap low, O'Toole stepped from the shack, strode up to the driver's side with authority and put a slug through the driver's nose. The back of the man's head filled the cab with gore. The second man jumped from the van and raised his rifle to fire. O'Toole shot him in the neck. Someone would have to clean the bloody uniform before it could be worn.

He pulled the dead driver to the back of the van, and then returned for the second corpse. His head was throbbing again. It was all he could do to manage to drag the third corpse from the shack.

The van was small. It would be a tight squeeze for eight, but it would have to do. The fuel gauge indicated it was half-full. Should do nicely, he decided. He pulled out and started back to the safehouse. Suddenly he spotted Nanos trudging along the road.

"What's in the bag?" he asked, pulling up beside the surprised Greek.

"Food, wonderful food." Alex opened the side door and climbed in.

"I see you managed three uniforms," he said, glancing behind his seat as they moved off.

"Did you have to speak Russian?" O'Toole asked.

"Not a bloody word."

"Me neither. Next time, they can send out Billy Two or Hayes. Piece of cake. Bloody Russian privates don't need to talk, anyway."

As he finished, he made the turn onto the road leading to the farm. They could barely make out the farmhouse even though the van's windshield wipers were going at full speed.

Inside everyone was dressed in dry clothes. The "liberated" Russian uniforms were quickly cleaned. O'Toole, Nanos and Sanchez, who had made his way back on foot, were resplendent in the uniforms. Each carried a loaded Kalashnikov slung over his shoulder.

The three bodies were weighted and thrown off the cliff. Hayes drove the van into the barn and cleaned out the mess. In the process he found a cache of hidden weapons. The most startling was an AGS-17 grenade launcher and three belts of ammunition. He'd heard of them but had never actually seen one.

Hayes's find was welcome. Dry and full, the SOBs were ready to fight. Barrabas was pleased with their progress. From a very bad situation, they had salvaged a great deal. He didn't want to waste any of the momentum. He gathered them around the stove.

"I want to get out of this area as soon as possible," he said. "The van will allow us to move inland. We have three Soviet uniforms and suitable identification. We're going to find the computer building today and retrieve what we came for. Any questions?"

"How do we find the building?" Hatton asked. "We don't have any maps."

"O'Toole lucked out. There were a couple in the car," he said, looking sideways at the big Irishman.

"Where do we stay? What kind of safehouse are we looking for?" Beck asked.

"We'll know when we see it, Nate," Barrabas said.

He looked around the table, from one face to another. His soldiers looked back at Barrabas, expressionlessly but with anticipation.

"Okay," he said. "Let's get this show on the road."

7

The bloodred sun began to set, changing the four-thousand-foot peaks of the island from blacks and dark grays to oranges and reds. Across Tatar Strait, the narrow waterway between mainland Russia and Sakhalin Island, the froth of churning water changed from white to red for the few minutes it took the fiery ball to disappear in the west.

At the narrow foot of the island opposite Hokkaido, the fleet of ships searching for the wreckage of the 747, turned on powerful lights as crew members watched for their divers to return. Bodies, carried by swirling currents, had been carried ashore on both islands for the past eight days.

His limousine passed scores of naval and salvage docks on the way home. But after a long and tiring day, Colonel Yuri Popolov's thoughts were not on the search for the jet. As the dockside smell of fuel and paint reached his nostrils, he was thinking of the coming evening. It was time for rest and recreation spent in the company of beautiful women.

Popolov had risen quickly in the KGB. A favorite of Andropov, he had retained favor after the man's death. He was six feet tall, 190 pounds, with blue eyes and brown hair. He was lean and fit and handsome in a hawklike way. He did not resemble his Slavic ancestors. His uniform was of the best quality, neatly pressed and changed every day in keeping with his fastidious nature. The man was also brilliant; he had to be to handle his new assignment. The colonel was not only in charge of security at the highly sensitive outpost, but was also allowed the freedom to involve the newly installed scientific community on the island in any intelligence plan he thought would confuse the West.

He had such a plan in the works—one that would cause the anxiety level in the White House to rise. The first step would be taken that same night.

Popolov's headquarters were in the capital city of Yuzhno-Sakhalinsk, south of Makarov, but his home was on the coast outside the small town of Novikovo. From the car, Popolov looked out on the rough water that separated Sakhalin Island from Hokkaido, the northern outpost of the Japanese island chain. He wondered if the Japanese living there felt the isolation, but his mind quickly returned to thoughts of the coming meeting.

The guards at his home saluted as the black limousine pulled up. The driver lowered a darkly tinted window. A brief examination of both the car's interior and the colonel's KGB identity card was acknowledged with a nod. The guards were thorough. They went through the routine every day, never permitting anyone, not even the master of the house, to enter without a careful screening. The limousine passed through high metal gates and drove up to the house, a two-story square structure—large but unimpressive.

The interior was luxurious, the overstuffed furniture and drapes of the finest velvets and brocades, the sculptures and paintings priceless.

The colonel enjoyed his isolation from Moscow. Yuzhno-Sakhalinsk, a relatively new outpost, had become a vital center for technical advancement. The island had recently been made the center for all computer installations and storage of technical research in the country. The most brilliant minds in the National Research Council had been transferred there. Soon the Politburo would include the base on their VIP tour list, and the dedicated Colonel Popolov would have to abandon his high living. He would have to resume the boring protocols, the posturing and again become the outspoken opponent of Western decadence that his rank demanded.

Once in his home, he placed a tray of vodka, ice and glasses on the table beside him. One bottle was half-empty. He spilled some of the alcohol on his lapels, scattered cigarette ash on his uniform and sat back in his chair with a half-filled glass in his hand.

A buzzer sounded from the front gate, and soon the front doorbell chimed. Popolov's manservant opened the door and ushered Anatole Persof inside. The short immaculately dressed man was a junior officer under Popolov's command. He was also the son of General Vladimir Persof, commander of all Afghan garrisons, a fact that he kept to himself. He did not want to be compared to his father. He knew that he couldn't measure up to the old man's standards. The younger

Persof was overweight, his Slavic face rounded and puffed. He was not a strong man and was easily intimidated by Popolov. He stopped just inside the door. Uncertainly, he approached the chair where Popolov sat.

"You were expecting me at eight?" he asked.

"Yes. Welcome, Persof. Sit, man! Sit and take some vodka," Popolov said, pouring the clear liquid into a glass.

"I am honored that you have asked me here, Colonel," a confused Persof said as he sat down. He had never been to the colonel's home.

"You are a good man, Anatole. I have kept an eye on you. No foolishness—all business. I like that." The dramatics should have been obvious, but Persof was unaware of the performance that was unfolding.

Persof preened. "I try to do my best, Colonel," he said, taking the first tentative drink from his glass.

"Call me Yuri. We should be better friends, Anatole. This is a lonely posting."

Persof knew it would be lonely for the KGB colonel who controlled the sensitive east coast. He had a similar problem. Agents of the KGB made few friends. "It is lonely work Col—Yuri." Person's tongue tripped over the familiarity. "Our work has eliminated the possibility of a social life."

Popolov wondered just how true this was in Persof's case. The man was an ass. "Drink up," he said, slurring the words. "Drink up. A toast to friendship." He spilled his drink as he raised it to his lips. His lapels were spotted with vodka and ash.

"How is the search going, Yuri? I get no news of it."

"I wish I could say the same. Our military friends are bunglers. They got themselves into the Korean mess. I don't feel sorry for them." The colonel sat forward, waving his drink as he spoke. "Soon we won't have to worry about the search. Soon we'll have the Americans in the trap." He began to laugh, spilling his drink again. He flopped back in his chair, stopped laughing and closed his eyes as if the vodka had taken its toll.

Persof waited, his surprise mounting. He had never seen the colonel like this.

Popolov opened his eyes.

"You were talking about the Americans being helpless," Persof reminded him, playing into the colonel's hand.

"I said that?" Popolov seemed alarmed, as if he'd betrayed a trust. Then he smiled, sat up in his chair and drained his glass.

Popolov seemed totally unlike the KGB chief his people saw every day. Persof sensed that something momentous was about to happen to him. He sat still, his heart pounding.

"When we have perfected it, they'll wish they'd never heard of us," Popolov almost shouted, with vodka spilling down his chin.

"Perfected what, Yuri?" Persof asked as he moved his chair closer.

Popolov looked at him through watery eyes. "The Afghan Snatch," he said, delighted with himself at the use of the American slang.

"You'll forgive my ignorance—" Persof was about to ask a question.

"Don't apologize, Anatole. How could you know? Oh, it's too good to be true!" He pounded a fist on the table, knocking the ice bucket to the floor.

Persof ignored the ice at his feet. He sat very still, willing the man to continue.

Through slitted eyes, Popolov saw the younger man's anxious gaze and knew what he was thinking. Persof was wondering if he would learn something about Afghanistan that would be helpful to his father. Popolov knew his act was working.

"The Afghan Snatch," he repeated, feigning slurred speech. "We are going to 'snatch' the Afghan rebel leaders. It's all set up. My cousin will take his Spetsnaz in and we'll put the Americans in the vise." He laughed aloud, choked on his vodka and coughed, hacking as the fiery liquid blazed down his windpipe.

It was obvious that Persof was trying not to show his impatience. The smell of spilled vodka and the colonel's breath were obviously affecting him. Cold sweat beaded across his forehead. He was in torment, impatient for his superior to continue.

"We will go in soon, perhaps as soon as five weeks. Six at the most. When we have the rebel leaders, we'll have the Yankees where we want them."

He could see that Persof was puzzled. He knew what was going through the man's mind. What would a simple kidnapping accomplish?

"You don't understand, do you?" Popolov flopped back into the deep chair. His glass crashed to the floor. As he grew closer to losing consciousness, he mumbled the last of his prepared speech. "My cousin Alexi Balandin will go in with his Spetsnaz. He'll take the rebel leaders, and the Americans will have three choices: they can come in to stop Balandin, in which case we will be waiting; they can ignore us again and be laughed at; or they can begin to supply arms to the Afghans, and we can brand them the aggressors. It's lovely—" he managed to get out before his head fell forward onto his chest.

Persof was obviously stunned. He sat for a full five minutes before rising and moving toward the door. Again it was opened by Popolov's manservant.

"He's had too much vodka," Persof said. He tried to appear calm as every nerve ending screamed at him.

"We'll leave him, Comrade," Popolov's employee said. "It is best we leave him when he's like this. The car will take you home."

As the door closed behind Persof, Gregor Urechek moved into his colonel's study. Popolov opened his eyes and started to laugh. "Did you see it?"

"On the monitor."

"Did he believe the story?"

"You were masterful, Colonel. A wonderful job of acting. He was actually shaking as he left."

"Good. He was an avid listener. He'll remember it well," Popolov said. "By tomorrow or the next day, General Persof will know of our supposed plan and will try to preempt us."

"What will be served in the end?" Gregor asked.

"Old Persof will look like a fool, and my chief will win another round in their long-standing feud."

"Is that all?"

"In Soviet politics, it is enough. One day my chief will be premier, and I will control the KGB. Politics, Gregor," Popolov said, turning for the stairs.

THE RAIN LET UP, but the rutted roads were quagmires that pulled at the van's wheels. Twice, in the middle of vast empty farm country, the SOBs had to pile out and push. Finally Barrabas ordered the tires deflated by a few pounds, and progress improved.

They could have taken the traveled roads, but almost every vehicle on them was military, and checkpoints were everywhere. On the back roads they ran into the odd checkpoint, but the guards checked the phony identification without enthusiasm, barely glancing at the driver and never looking inside the van.

By 1700 hours, they were at the outskirts of Makarov, on Sakhalin's coast. To find it, they had to cross through the mountain passes that ribbed the center of the island.

It was obvious that the town had once been a fishing village. Military installations and huge blocklike structures stood beside old wooden wharves and warehouses. A forest of masts still bobbed in the chop of the harbor.

Sanchez, their best linguist, drove most of the way. He steered the mud-splattered van along the narrow seashore road among the old buildings. Hangouts for the local fishermen dotted the street on the waterfront. Seamen staggered from their favorite drinking spots.

The last warehouse at the north end of the street looked deserted. Sanchez pulled around to the side.

O'Toole deftly picked the lock, and they drove the van inside. The smell of fish, the legions of scaled swimmers hauled from the sea and passed over the filleting tables, rose up to punish their nostrils.

The building was about sixty feet square. One of its two rooms contained several stone-topped filleting tables, the other had been converted into living quarters for one man. The small room contained a bed and a small set of drawers. The large room had no ceiling and the joists loomed over the SOBs' heads. It was old, but it was dry and would serve their purposes.

"We need seamen's clothes for Nanos and Sanchez. Look around and see what you can find," Barrabas commanded. While they rummaged through the old wood structure, he slipped outside and looked over their position.

Darkness was just beginning to fall on the fishing village. Barrabas climbed the hill rising from the other side of the street. The road to the north continued as far as he could see. To the south, the road followed the contour of the harbor. They had a few choices, he concluded, if they needed to get out in a hurry.

His warriors had turned on a few lights in their search, but they could hardly be seen in the gloom that surrounded the harbor. A fog was beginning to roll in.

Back inside, Barrabas saw Sanchez and Nanos going through a pile of clothing.

"Someone lives here. One man. He's of middle height, weighs about a hundred and eighty, is broad-shouldered and has a potbelly," Lee told Barrabas. "He smokes, keeps a good supply of vodka on hand and eats out."

"No food."

"Right."

"Sanchez and Nanos will have to bring in food. Better get something we don't have to heat," Barrabas said.

"It looks like the clothes will fit," Nanos said. "This is my meat. Talk of fish and boats is the same the world over. What about our friend?" He pointed to Sanchez.

"Don't worry about me, man," Sanchez replied, his generous mustache moving with his lips as he talked, then smiled. "I've done my share of marine work. I'll concentrate on the food this time. You go for the information. That okay with you, Colonel?"

"Should work. Make it an hour. One hour, and I'll send O'Toole after you. Try to get what we need as close to this place as possible," he said. "Okay. Let's move it."

Nanos, in blue jeans, a pea jacket and a black toque, was the classic seaman. Sanchez, in dark blue coveralls and a blue cardigan, left his polished dome bare. His appearance was not that different from men they'd seen weaving along the streets before dark.

Barrabas opened the door and the two men stepped out.

8

The inside of the warehouse was alive with activity. Sanchez returned with a huge pot of hot borscht he'd stolen from a little restaurant kitchen down the street. He went back for a couple of loaves of bread, sneaked them out while the owner was out front shouting at his few patrons, trying to find out who had stolen the soup. Sanchez knew the owner wouldn't call the authorities. That would make more trouble for him than the thieves already had.

Nanos drank vodka with a group of sailors and learned which one lived in the warehouse at the end of the street. He gently led the drunken man to the building, where they were confronted by seven pairs of foreign eyes. It almost sobered the drunken sailor.

O'Toole grabbed the wiry Russian from behind, clamped a hand over his mouth and whispered menacingly into his ear, "Do not try to shout. You will not be harmed if you remain calm." He paused for a moment, twisting the man's arm up in a viselike grip. "I'm going to take my hand from your mouth. If you cry out, we will kill you. We have nothing to lose."

Billy Two loomed behind O'Toole, ready to silence the man if he shouted.

O'Toole released him. The sailor stood, speechless, looking around at the group. Five of them were still dressed for battle, complete with weapons. He moved to a chair and sat down, shaking his head, trying to clear away the effect of the vodka.

Nanos, O'Toole and Sanchez pulled up chairs in front of him. They sat there until he looked up.

"What do you want from me?" he asked.

"We will stay here for a few hours. We will not harm you. We will leave the place as we found it," Sanchez said, trying to keep the language as simple as possible.

"I don't understand. Why my place?"

"That does not matter," O'Toole said. "Where is the building housing the new computers?" he asked.

"Why do you want to know?" The man was starting to sober up. Frightened, he began to shake.

"Bring him a bowl of borscht," Nanos called over his shoulder. It would give the man something to do with his hands and would maybe calm him.

"We will ask the questions. Where is the new computer building?" O'Toole repeated.

The man's lined face stiffened as he looked into the eyes of the Irishman and saw death. He looked at the other two and saw the same expression. The others were sitting on chairs or on the floor, cleaning their weapons or looking at him.

"Tell us, Comrade," Sanchez urged, trying to eliminate any trace of menace from his voice.

Beck placed a small table between the four men and a bowl of steaming soup in front of the seaman.

"I can't talk good. I could maybe draw a picture," the man said through a spoonful of soup.

Beck had gone through all the drawers in the living quarters and was sitting with a pad and pencil, making a list of the things he planned to do in the computer room.

With a pencil, the man scrawled on the paper. The result showed the shoreline, several squares that might be buildings, and some ships. One building, larger than the rest, had been filled in with the dull black pencil.

"How many streets to the building?" O'Toole asked.

"From where?"

"From here to this corner," O'Toole pointed to one of the streets on the map.

The man stopped eating to think. He counted in his head, gave it up, and started with his grimy left hand. Running out of fingers, he started on his right. "Seven streets," he said.

"How many from here to the building?" Again O'Toole pointed to the intersection seven blocks from where they sat.

The man had a mouthful of the fresh bread. He tried to talk through it and gave up, spent time thinking, trying to see the streets in his mind.

"I don't know. Maybe six, maybe eight. Across the street is a place where they save old metal. Two cranes work in the yard moving the metal around," he said, now more comfortable, enjoying the borscht. A trickle of beet juice stained one corner of his beard.

"The color of the building where the computers are?" Nanos asked.

"Yellow. It is yellow. All the new ones are red brick, but this one is yellow."

Barrabas came over and whispered in O'Toole's ear.

"Are you sure it's the one with computers?" the Irishman asked. "Do you know what a computer is?"

"The fish have not been running. I helped unload some trucks. One of the men said the crates held computers."

"What do you think?" O'Toole asked the other two in English. "Is that the building we want?" He pointed to the block on the map.

"Seven blocks south and about eight blocks inland," Nanos said. "Yeah. I think we can go with that."

Barrabas had been listening to the exchange. "Let's do it."

"Why don't the three of us cruise around in our uniforms and look it over?" O'Toole suggested. "I'd like to make sure we've got the right place, then come back for you."

"No. Sounds like standard procedure, but nothing is going to go by the book," Barrabas said. "Every time we open those doors and drive out, someone from the military might see. We go out once and come back once."

"Lee," Barrabas called.

"Colonel?"

"I want you to baby-sit this man." He pointed at the seaman who had finished the soup and was contentedly puffing away on a pipe. "I'm taking everyone but you to the computer building. I want you available with your drugs if we bring someone back. You're our lookout here," he said. "Got that?"

"Got it."

"All right. Gather around." Barrabas waved them all in. "This is how we'll do it."

THE BLACK VAN PULLED OUT of the warehouse just after 2200 hours. Sanchez drove again, with O'Toole sitting up front. Barrabas crouched between them, memorizing everything he saw.

Sanchez drove carefully along the fogbound harbor road for seven blocks and turned inland. After six blocks the fog lifted, and they saw the yellow brick building with the scrap metal yard across the street. Two sentries were on duty beneath a string of low-powered bulbs. Except for the fluorescent light spilling from the upper floors, the street was in shadow.

"Drive past," Barrabas said. "I want to explore the streets around here for a few blocks. We may have to circle back if we attract any attention."

The headlights cut through the blackness, free from fog above the shoreline. After four blocks the road narrowed into a rutted lane like the one they'd used on their way in.

"Try the streets to the north," he suggested.

The first three were the same as the first. The fourth was asphalt leading into the mountains and toward the west coast.

"Can anyone read those signs?" Barrabas asked.

O'Toole, Nanos and Sanchez squinted in the uncertain light.

"The top one is Krasnogorsk," Sanchez said. "The smaller one at the bottom is Il'inskiy. It looks like it's an airport. Let me see the map."

The map was passed forward. It, too, was in Russian. "Yeah. Il'inskiy. Definitely an airport," he said.

"How far?" Barrabas asked.

"Five miles as the crow flies. Probably ten or fifteen over the mountain," Sanchez said.

"Everybody get that?" Barrabas asked. "We might need to know later."

Everyone gave an acknowledgment.

They drove through back streets and ended up at the warehouse again. It looked quiet and was almost in complete darkness. Retracing the route to the seventh block south, Barrabas pointed out another sign.

"Bykov twenty miles, Dolinsk twenty-five, Yuzhno-Sakhalinsk thirty and Novikovo thirty-five," Sanchez again translated.

"What's the Sakhalinsk one?" Barrabas asked.

"The capital."

"And Novikovo. What's the small print beneath it?"

Sanchez rolled down the window and squinted to read the sign. "Apparently it's a private community. Russia's classless society has private villages for the VIPs. I'd say Novikovo would be it."

"Okay. Enough recon. Let's do it," Barrabas said.

Sanchez drove as if he were out for a Sunday drive. At the computer building, he pulled up slowly and then shouted out the window. "Don't come to us, comrades. We'll come to you." To O'Toole, he said, "It's a vodka scam. Follow my lead."

The other SOBs watched in silence as Sanchez slipped from one door and O'Toole departed through the other. They didn't know what their friends were saying, but the guards seemed interested.

"Don't come into the light, Comrades. Vodka from home. Good stuff," Sanchez said, his approach smooth, reassuring. "No point in advertising to the world. We've only got a few bottles."

O'Toole and Sanchez walked slowly toward the guards, who held their AK-47s in combat readiness. Their hands slipped inside their greatcoats as if for the vodka. As soon as they stepped into darkness, they drew their Berettas. Their shots punched holes in each startled face. They left the Russians where they lay.

When Barrabas saw them saunter out of the shadows with the guards' AK-47s slung over their shoulders, he backed the truck up to the side of the building and parked in the shadows. O'Toole and Sanchez came up, assuming the roles of the Russians they had killed.

"Okay, O'Toole. You and Sanchez get those dead guards under cover. Billy, I want a recon of the whole circumference. If there are other guards, hide them well."

William Starfoot II crept from the van, despite his size. Moccasins or paratrooper boots, it made no difference, he moved without sound.

He circled from front to back, from north to south. Directly in back of the building, about fifty feet from the foundation wall, he saw something move among the young trees that had grown to shoulder height since the building's construction.

A sentry.

Billy Two moved slowly. It took a minute to reach a position behind the man, close enough to hear him breathe. The SOB carried his commando knife in his teeth, preferring to stalk with his hands free.

The Russian turned and brought his weapon up to bear. In one motion, Billy drew the knife from his mouth, reached out and spun the man around, and grasping his chin with his left hand, put a knee in the small of the man's back and slashed his throat. The sharp steel cut through to bone.

The only sound was the rush of blood on leaves and gravel. When it was done, he moved through the young maples and back to the van.

"One sentry, Colonel," he reported. "They will not find him back there."

"All right. Let's get with it," Barrabas said.

He motioned for Claude Hayes, who had been in the shadows talking to O'Toole, to join him. "You set up near the back door. If anyone comes out that way, I want them dead. When it's over, I'll send Billy for you."

When Hayes snaked through the young growth of trees to his post, the four SOBs donned gas masks. Like inhuman forms, they slipped through the front door and into the lower hallway. They all had their Socimi rifles and Berettas, in addition to their special supplies.

They had no time for cutting communications or looking for a central air control. Billy Two would smash a canister at both ends of each hallway. Barrabas and Nanos would cover the hallways as Billy worked. Beck would keep his eyes peeled for the master computer console. They moved as quietly as possible.

It went well for the first three floors. On the fourth, a guard, unaffected by the gas, reached for his rifle. Nanos hit him with a 3-round burst of 9 mm slugs. The guard went down, but not before his automatic rifle stitched a row of holes along the floor near Billy and up the wall to the ceiling.

The noise was deafening.

In the upper hallway, the four SOBs froze.

"I see it!" Nate Beck called out. He had traveled ten thousand miles for his golden fleece, and he'd just found it—the treasured console.

"Billy. You stick with Nate. Alex and I will do a recon of the lower floors. I want to make sure everyone down there is knocked out."

The two men, accustomed to each other's movements, covered all four floors thoroughly. In the whole building, they found six people—the dead guard, two more who were knocked out and three unconscious scientists sitting at desks. None of the scientists had a telephone off the hook or looked as though he'd had time to call anyone.

They'd found one of the unconscious scientists in what seemed to be the biggest office. Barrabas wondered if they had struck it rich. He called for Nanos, shouting through the mask. Damn! They should have had communicators, he thought to himself. They should have had a lot of other things, but they didn't.

"Can you read this guy's title?" he asked through the clumsy mask.

"I'm not great at reading the stuff, Colonel. I think he's the director of research, but I can't be sure."

"Relieve Sanchez and send him up here right away," Barrabas said.

While he waited, Barrabas looked over the floor he was on. It was the second of four. Billy and Alex were on the fourth. Everywhere he looked, he saw computers and computer tapes. Wall shelving was filled with magnetic tapes, thousands of them within his sight. Perhaps a hundred thousand within the building. It was awesome.

Sanchez looked strange in his gas mask. It wasn't the best fit for a man with a mustache as large as his. "What is it you want me to read, Colonel?" he asked.

"This man's title." Barrabas pointed toward the huge man sprawled across the desk.

"Director general of research. His name is Fedesoff." Sanchez pulled the man from the desk, reached inside his coat pocket and pulled out a wallet. "Same name. This is your top guy, Colonel."

"I'm going up to the top floor," Barrabas said. "I'll send Billy down to put this one in the van and to stay with him. When Billy's gone, you come upstairs. Nate may have trouble with the language. He's a bloody whiz with a computer, but he may be stymied by the Russian."

Barrabas took the stairs two at a time, and found a frustrated Nate pounding on the console desk.

"Billy. Go to the second floor and find Sanchez," Barrabas said through the mask. "Take his prisoner to the car and hold him until we're finished here."

Billy didn't have to be told twice. Nate looked up at his colonel with eyes filled with frustration.

"I've got it all, Colonel. I've opened up this sucker like a ripe peach, but I don't know what I've got. Look at this," he said, pointing to a clear graphics layout. "This must be the plans for their newest aircraft. This one looks like a new nuclear submarine. I've even got the plans for their next missile cruiser— I think. But I can't be sure of anything."

"What about their intelligence system? Can we find out who ordered the 747 down?"

"Nothing, Colonel. I wouldn't have known what these things were if I hadn't seen the damned diagrams."

"Sit tight. Sanchez is on his way up. You two should be able to decipher most of it."

"Should help, but I've got some more bad news. I can't get it out by modem. Everything is encoded out of here. There's no way it would get past their monitor system."

"Okay. So we carry it out. What are we talking about?"

"A couple of magnetic tapes. No sweat, but it would have been sweeter to have sent it out and know it got there."

"What the hell does that mean?"

"I'm not chicken, Colonel. You know that. This place is weird, that's all. In the Cambodian jungles I never felt totally cut off. But this place...I don't know."

"It's okay, Nate. I suspect we're all feeling like that right now. Most of us won't admit it."

Sanchez walked into the room and sat beside Nate. He seemed to know instinctively what had to be done. Barrabas would have liked to give them unlimited time, but he, too, had a funny feeling. They'd been damned lucky. More than they deserved. Up till now, they had been shadows in a fortress considered impenetrable. Their action tonight would change that.

"One hour, Nate. If you can't find the intelligence files by then, that's it. Put what you can on tape and we'll take it out."

At exactly 0200 hours, Barrabas told Billy to round up the bodies of the dead guards and carry them to the truck. Nanos watched over the prisoners. With the Greek at the wheel, they drove to a deserted quarry, weighted the bodies with limestone secured by rusty baling wire and dropped the dead Russians into the muddy water.

Half an hour later Barrabas called off the computer search. The three SOBs cleaned up the place to confuse the Russian authorities, then left to join the others. Nate carried two tapes of vital information, but nothing on the Korean jet.

9

Yuzhno-Sakhalinsk was once the sleepy capital of a remote east-coast island. The principle industry had been fishing. Farming and fishing made the island self-sufficient. A town council, duly elected, despite complaints by party representatives to Moscow, had built a magnificent town hall. Magnificent by Sakhalin standards.

The center of the town featured a square copied from a decadent American magazine, one that depicted "middle America." They called it Groman Square after the town's first mayor. A huge grassy area had been the basis for the landscaping, and in its center they had built a bandstand, just like the one in the picture. On Sundays and holidays, the town band used to play for the people who would gather in the tranquil setting to relax. Moscow and the burden of communism were far away.

But that peaceful era seemed so long ago. Progress had come to Yuzhno-Sakhalinsk, and with progress came Colonel Yuri Popolov.

The square was now bare. The bandstand had been torn down, the grass removed and the square paved. Every foot of the square had been paved. And it had

been renamed. To satisfy the perverse ego of Popolov, it was now called Dzerzhinsky Square, the same
as the notorious square where the offices of the Komitet Gosudarstvennoi Bezopasnosti, the hated KGB,
were located in Moscow.

The town hall had become Popolov's headquarters, with the front sandblasted and an unattractive
block addition added. The cellars were now used for
less tranquil pursuits than under the succession of
peace-loving mayors.

Yuzhno-Sakhalinsk had fallen under hard times and
the iron fist of "the Colonel." It was even rumored
that many of the island's most attractive women had
disappeared, and behind closed doors people's fingers pointed at Popolov.

The second floor of the old city hall, with its oversize bay windows, had been renovated to resemble the
office of the KGB chief in Moscow. Popolov rea-
soned that he should become accustomed to those
surrounding, since he would be in that exalted office
one day. He ran the whole island, including the military, as if he already held the rank. Everyone shrank
before him. He had powerful friends in Moscow—
friends one would not want to cross.

The morning after his meeting with Persof, he sat in
his office examining three reports on his desk. His face
was livid. He reached for his intercom and punched a
button.

"Have Nekrasov and Obolensky arrived?" he
screamed.

"They are with me, Colonel," his aide answered, his voice reflecting the fear that he lived with twenty-four hours a day.

"Send them in, you fool. What the hell are you waiting for?"

The massive carved doors swung open, and two officers marched in smartly. Colonel Boris Nekrasov, military commander of the Sakhalin garrison and overall commander of its defenses, stood before his desk. He was of equal rank, had served with distinction, but was no match for Popolov. Rank meant little in the Soviet military in the face of political influence. Major Gavrill Obolensky, Popolov's second-in-command, a young man with a future who had asked for his present posting, also stood rigidly. Both men were accustomed to Popolov's eccentricities, but dared not oppose him in any way.

"Do you see these reports? As we sit here on this fortified island, this bastion of Soviet power, we are being infiltrated. What do you know of this?" Popolov asked.

"I have read the reports, Colonel," Obolensky said, his voice calm. He did not fear Popolov but respected him, took the abuse and kept his cool. "I have ordered everyone on the island questioned."

"And you, Nekrasov. These reports concern you," Popolov said, not disguising the contempt he felt for the military man. "Twenty men killed on the beach at Mys Aniva. Three of your people disappear up the coast from Mys Krilon. Four guards at the most important computer storage building in the Soviet disappear. These are the people Moltsov confessed to helping. What does all that tell you, Nekrasov?''

"That we have been breached, Colonel," he replied.

"Sit! You might as well sit. This could take some time." He pulled a gold case from his tunic, tamped a monogrammed cigarette from the case and lit it with a gold Dunhill.

"We have been breached. The infiltrators, whoever they are, are still here," Popolov said, blowing smoke directly at his military counterpart. "What the hell are you doing about it?

"I have canceled all leaves, doubled security," Nekrasov said. "At first, I thought we had beaten off the invaders at Mys Aniva. We found a deflated rubber raft at the beach. But it is now obvious that they crossed the bay at Zaliv Aniva and climbed the cliffs up the coast. My people found a second inflatable sunk in ten feet of water and a deserted farmhouse at the top of the cliff had obviously been used." He took a silver case from his tunic, extracted a small Havana cigar, bit off the end, lit it and blew smoke across the desk.

"Is that all?" Popolov demanded.

"Three of my missing men are from the same region. A van is also missing. It will carry an absolute maximum of ten men," Nekrasov continued. "Unless they are on foot, we are dealing with an elite force of ten men or less."

"That tallies with what I have, Colonel," Obolensky interrupted. "The break-in at the computer center suggests they traveled overland quickly. They either had to steal a second vehicle, and we have no such report, or they were limited to ten men."

"Do you realize what they might have taken from our computer files?" Popolov asked. "With a computer whiz and knowledge of our language, they could have compromised almost any project."

"Fortunately I set up our department files on a separate system," Obolensky offered. Like Popolov, he was never one to miss an opportunity.

"And you, Nekrasov. Were you as farsighted?" Popolov asked.

"All our fleet plans, fortifications—everything in my command—are on file at the center." He drew in smoke and breathed it out erratically. "I am concerned the most with the files on National Research. We have all our space technology, our chemical warfare advances—everything."

"I have three other minor reports, two from Makarov and one from a farmer on the west coast. It seems the invaders stole enough food to feed about a dozen people not three miles from the guard post where your men disappeared." Popolov looked at Nekrasov over a pair of reading glasses.

"At Makarov, we have a sailor who didn't report for duty and who can't be found. And then there is a restaurant manager complaining that a caldron of borscht was stolen last night." Popolov looked at Obolensky. "Not important when taken singularly, but together they spell the presence of invaders not a mile from the computer storage." He looked at his assistant with disdain. "It is detail that will make you a success, Obolensky, or leave you to stagnate." He smoked for a few seconds, letting the thought sink in.

"Don't you suppose it would be a good idea to investigate these two minor incidents before our unwelcome guests venture out again?" Popolov looked from one man to the other, then waved a hand.

"Dismissed," he said, then swiveled in his chair to look out on the square below.

THE WAREHOUSE CAME TO LIFE at 0300 hours.

"Did we get it?" Lee asked as the SOBs poured from the van.

"No. I don't think it's on their banks," Beck said dejectedly. "I picked out a lot of vital stuff, but nothing on their intelligence system and nothing on the KAL flight."

"We've got a patient for you, Lee," Barrabas said. "This is one Alexi Fedesoff, the director general of research at the computer and science center." He pointed to the limp body Billy Two was carrying to a filleting table by a far wall. "Get what you can out of him."

"What's to eat?" Nanos, the perpetually hungry Greek, asked.

"Can't take a chance on another raid, Alex," Barrabas said, tossing him a candy bar.

"Where'd you get these?" Nanos asked.

"The director's desk. The guy had a whole carton—a real sweet tooth." Barrabas walked around the group, tossing a bar to each.

When he got to Lee, she waved off the offer, already wrapped up in her work. "I'm going to need

Sanchez on this. I've got to get Fedesoff ready, then ask one hell of a lot of questions," she said.

"Does he have to be conscious before you start?" Barrabas asked.

"It would help, but we don't have time, do we?" she asked, with a knowing look in her eye. Lee had been through the mill long before she'd ever met Barrabas. Walker Jessup knew her background when he'd forced her on Barrabas for their first mission. Her medical skills had been needed then, and they were needed now.

"No. Time we do not have," Barrabas replied. "Do the best you can, Lee. When we've finished with him, we either get out, or we have new work to do. It's up to you." He left her and went to the back of the warehouse to get Sanchez.

Sanchez and Nanos knelt at a rusted trapdoor in the cement floor. The Greek held a rusty prying bar that he'd found in the seaman's toolbox. He was cleaning the edges of the trapdoor and trying to pry it open.

"Lee needs you to help with the interrogation, José," Barrabas said, never taking his eyes off the work in progress. "I'll send Hayes over to help you with that." He didn't know what Nanos had in mind, but he wasn't about to interrupt the work.

Barrabas was concerned with their situation. No place was safe for more than a few hours, and they had outlived their time frame on this one. As soon as Lee was finished, they would have to take off, probably for the airport at Il'inskiy.

On one of the filleting slabs, Billy Two and O'Toole laid out the hardware they had captured from the

Russians. They had seven AK-47s and the unique AGS-17 grenade launcher that was belt-fed. They had three belts for the weapon, although Barrabas was leery of using it because field tests had reported that it was unreliable.

Beside the battered old launcher, Billy Two laid out an RPG-7 Rocket Propelled Grenade. It would be useful against a troop carrier or a small armored vehicle. Useful, but he hoped they'd never run into anything as formidable.

Nanos and Hayes had the trapdoor open and had disappeared down the a rusty old ladder to the water below. Barrabas had no intention of keeping track of them. They were looking for a back exit.

Time passed slowly. Hatton's work was painstakingly slow. Nanos and Hayes returned, apparently satisfied with the route they'd found. The old seaman slept through dawn and the first few hours of daylight.

The sea was warm, although the air was still cool. A mist floated across the top of the water, but the air was clear above. Barrabas was ready to call off Hatton's work and get them on the road again.

"Colonel!" Hatton called from the other side of the warehouse.

Barrabas made it over there in seconds. "What have you got?"

"I'm going to take him through it again to confirm. Sanchez will translate," she said, turning to Sanchez with the first question.

"Who gave the order to shoot down the Korean aircraft?"

The answer was slow in coming, the enunciation slurred. "The man who runs everyone's life here," the Russian said. Although he was technically unconscious, his emotions were quite evident. He apparently hated the man.

"What is this man's name?" she whispered to Sanchez, who spoke into the scientist's ear.

"Colonel Yuri Popolov," the scientist said with a sneer on his face.

"Where do we find this colonel?" she asked.

"His headquarters are in Yuzhno-Sakhalinsk," came the reply.

Barrabas whispered in Hatton's ear.

"Where does he live? Where does he sleep at night?" Sanchez relayed as the others began to gather around.

"The monster has a house down the coast at Novikovo," the Russian answered.

"That's the town I told you would be for VIPs," Sanchez reminded Barrabas.

"That's just great, Lee," Barrabas said. "It means we can still get the information we came for if we can isolate Popolov. I'd like to get the hell out of here— find a new safehouse. We've pressed our luck here."

"Wait, Colonel," Lee urged. "One more thing— and it might be important."

She asked one more question, and Sanchez whispered the translation into the man's ear. At first Fedesoff resisted. It was something he protected, but finally the combined drugs Lee had given him won out.

"The computer and science center is a depository for all Soviet developments over the past five years. The master plan calls for a second depository to be built in a secret place, a backup, but the funds for such a project have not been allocated."

The SOBs were silent for a few seconds, then Beck whistled. "This is bigger than the KAL thing. My God, if we could destroy the building, we could set them back five or ten years—everything they've got."

Everyone started to talk at once. The computer center had to be the prime target. Destroy it and clear out. It made sense.

"We were paid to find out who ordered the KAL flight shot down and why," Barrabas said, overriding the group.

"Popolov has the answers. We go after him. If we are successful with Popolov, we can still go for the computer center, okay." Barrabas looked around the group. "But the colonel that Fedesoff seems to hate is our number one priority."

Without warning, an explosion rocked the building.

10

No more than a second had passed before every SOB went into action. The old warehouse was under attack. Someone had decided to shoot first and talk later. The enemy was shredding the outer walls with bullets from a dozen automatic rifles.

"The tables!" Barrabas shouted.

The tops of the filleting tables were four inches of thick, smooth stone. Billy Two and O'Toole cleared the weapons from one table and upended it, then slid weapons and clips across the cement floor to their colleagues. Nanos and Hayes tipped a table over in front of their exit hatch and opened the creaking steel door.

The enemy lobbed grenades at the roof, and a steady hail of spent shards of steel rained down on the SOBs, some drawing blood. Billy Two shoved a belt into the AGS-17 and lobbed a stream of grenades through the openings between the rafters with accuracy. He couldn't afford to miss his target.

Barrabas helped Beck tip over one of the tables, took an AK-47 in his hands and fired short bursts through gaps in the wall at the enemy he couldn't see.

The enemy ceased fire. A bullhorn sounded in the silence that followed.

"Drop your weapons and come out!" The accent was Russian, the message universal.

O'Toole crept to a corner where some fragments of wood remained. He dragged the RPG-7 after him, then lay flat on the floor with the tube over his right shoulder, and aimed at the armored truck where the commands were coming from.

Leaving a trail of gray smoke behind, the rocket streaked toward the truck. In a millisecond the vehicle mushroomed into a ball of orange flame. Metal and scraps of torn flesh rained down on the enemy.

O'Toole was the only one ready for the blast. He reloaded the devastating tube with his last rocket grenade, and in the light from the burning truck, he picked out another target.

Most of the enemy were positioned on their bellies around a troop carrier they had pulled up to block the road. With a deadly whoosh of sound and a trail of gray smoke, the second grenade hit the troop carrier and tore it into thousands of shards of metal that caught the enemy in a spray of sharp steel. The ruptured fuel tank rained burning gas on everyone within twenty feet. The result was carnage.

The sickly smell of burning flesh drifted into the warehouse. Barrabas and Beck were the first to follow with a hail of steel-jacketed bullets at the now-illuminated targets. The sailor, who cowered in a corner, chose that moment to run screaming across the room toward the safety of his living quarters—an upturned bed and mattress, anything to escape the living hell.

The enemy poured a barrage of metal at the shattered warehouse, but it was a poor imitation of their first assault. The sailor was caught by dozens of slugs that picked him up, danced him between the tables and flung him against the far wall.

Billy Two answered the barrage with the AGS-17. He could see the enemy now as he placed his shots. One of the small grenades hit a rafter, shattering the wood, sending lead and splinters down on everyone.

None of the SOBs had escaped the barrage of steel pouring down on them. Luckily the pieces had been small, although rips in their jump suits attested to direct hits on Kevlar or wounds where the armored vests didn't afford protection.

Hayes and Nanos returned to guide the others out. Hayes frog-walked to the table where Hatton was pouring slugs from her captured Russian rifle.

"Get out, Lee," he shouted in her ear and pointed to the hatch.

He turned to Sanchez, who was picking off individual targets with a Socimi. "Go down with Lee, José. We'll follow, two at a time."

Sanchez broke off and followed Lee down the hatch.

Barrabas and Beck shared one barricade. Bullets chipped away at the stone slabs, bringing death a half inch closer with every hit. They had very little ammunition left and were on single shot with the Socimis and AK-47s. It seemed like a one-sided futile effort.

Behind their table, O'Toole and Billy Two adopted the same approach. They fired single rounds, throwing used magazines and weapons aside when they were no longer useful, taking the battle down to the last shell.

The enemy fire, though less heavy than at first, continued to be a rain of steel they could not escape. As the firefight drew to its seemingly inevitable conclusion, the firing came from a different quarter, tearing away the last remnants of the front wall and revealing the unconscious scientist on his bed of stone. Slugs tore at his flesh, carrying him from the table to the floor. His corpse joined the pulverized remains of the seaman.

The stink of gore filled the warehouse. Three tables, close together, shielded the trapdoor where Nanos, Hatton and Sanchez had disappeared. The tables would not protect them much longer. If O'Toole and Billy Two had not silenced the enemy grenade launchers, all of the SOBs would have been killed, drummed into pulp by hundreds of rounds of steel and lead.

Hayes crept to Barrabas's position. "Three down the hatch, Colonel," he said. "Who'll give cover fire?"

"Get O'Toole and Billy out. Nate and I will cover."

Hayes crept to the table covering the Indian and the redhead. "Down the hatch!" he yelled over the enemy fire. "Colonel's orders!"

Hayes followed O'Toole and Billy Two down the ladder to a rotting wooden platform and an ancient fishing boat. Nanos had the old diesel on idle. Sanchez collected all of the remaining weapons—a pitiful collection of arms with very little ammunition.

Billy Two and Liam joined the motley crew, leaving only Barrabas and Beck above. It was very dark after the flashes of gunfire and the bright flash of flame. When their night vision improved, they could see that no one among them had escaped injury.

Hayes climbed down the ladder, followed by Beck and finally, Barrabas. They cast off, and Nanos steered the craft at low revs through a forest of rotting pilings below neighboring warehouses.

The chatter of small arms faded behind them.

MAJOR OBOLENSKY STOOD among the ruins of his attack force, unable to believe that so few invaders had been able to fight back with such force. But their fire had gradually diminished. It would soon be over. He would be victorious.

He had been in touch with the colonel, who'd felt no need to leave his house. Obolensky had not reported the loss of the vehicles or the twoscore men killed. The battle would have been over much sooner had the enemy not destroyed his grenade launchers. If the warehouse had not been attached to a row of wood structures, some occupied by the good people of Makarov, he would have used phosphorus grenades and fried the enemy for their bold venture onto Sakhalin soil.

He had intended only to watch and command as necessary, but when his military captain was killed by the first rocket grenade, he took over. Popolov insisted that the whole team of invaders be eliminated.

He would have preferred a prisoner or two for interrogation but Popolov sometimes let his blood lust cloud his judgment. If anyone survived, Obolensky would handle the interrogation himself, and the facts would be fed back to Moscow, adding to the nails he was secretly hammering into Popolov's coffin.

The firing had ceased in the warehouse. All Obolensky could see through the smoke and the fog now drifting in was a skeleton of a building and a number of stone slabs perpendicular to the floor. Through night glasses, he spotted two bodies against the back wall. He figured that the rest of the enemy force was probably lying dead behind the stone slabs.

Major Gavrill Obolensky ordered his troops to cease firing. No fire was returned from the warehouse. It was a derelict skeleton, his for the taking.

Three men followed their sergeant through the stink of death, picking their way from one piece of rubble to the next. They sprayed the inside of the building with a steady flow of slugs until their magazines were empty.

Obolensky followed them down the fifty feet of road to the ruined building. It was dark. He couldn't see more than a few feet ahead. The two bodies against the wall were Russian. He recognized the illustrious scientist. He saw no one else.

Somehow the enemy had escaped. But the worst part of the night was yet to come. He had to report to Popolov.

THEY MOVED SLOWLY and cautiously beneath the jutting piers of the harborfront warehouses for a half mile. Nanos finally took them into a jetty out in the open beyond the warehouses. A rolling fog hung only a few feet above the water.

The cement jetty was new, built to serve a new warehouse. They climbed the steps leading to the warehouse. A group of curious citizens crowded the street closer to the firefight. They could still hear some sporadic firing.

Sanchez picked the lock of the huge steel door and pulled it to one side. Inside, the walls were lined with steel filleting tables. In the center of the huge space, three trucks stood ready for work the next day—box vans, filled with baskets that stank of fish.

No one had to issue orders. Beck and Sanchez started to unload the baskets from the truck closest to the front door. Nanos was in the cab, reaching under the dash for the ignition wires.

Most of them had been hit, but no one was seriously hurt. The Kevlar had protected them.

O'Toole and Billy Two hauled open the rolling doors and peered out. Everyone was still occupied by the sporadic firing that continued up the street. Billy signaled to Sanchez behind the wheel and the Latin American drove the truck through the doors. They all jumped on except Billy, who pulled the warehouse doors closed before boarding.

Barrabas was up front with Sanchez and O'Toole. A sliding panel opened to the back. Sanchez flicked the inside light on and found a switch for the rear dome light before turning off the one in the cab.

"Head past the computer building so we can find the road leading to Il'inskiy," Barrabas said. "I'd like to put about twenty miles or more between us and that warehouse.''

"Let's look for an occupied farmhouse this time," O'Toole suggested. "We can't afford to go out foraging for food. We should also take care of any injuries we've sustained."

"You been hit, Liam?" Barrabas asked.

"A couple of pieces of steel in one ankle. It's not bleeding now."

Sanchez said nothing as he peered out at the black night, trying to read road signs that were few and far between. A trickle of blood ran down his forehead from a long cut. A piece of shrapnel had knocked off his Kevlar skullcap and another had missed scalping him by a whisker. He had small pieces of shrapnel in each ankle and huge bruises under the Kevlar where he had been punched by small-caliber slugs.

In a half hour they crossed over the peaks of the low mountains that formed a spine down the center of the island and were tearing down the leeward side toward Il'inskiy. The airport flashed past a few minutes later as their headlights cut a pathway of light through a sheet of rain that had begun a few miles back.

"Turn in one of these back roads," Barrabas ordered. "I've seen three since we passed the airport."

Sanchez nodded and slowed, peering through the flashing windshield wipers to see the turn-off. He turned inland and east up a rutted road. They drove three miles until the land began sloping upward again before they saw a dull glow of light coming from a farmhouse window.

Sanchez cut the headlights and drove slowly to the side of the house. Barrabas and O'Toole rushed the front and back doors, kicked their way inside, their Socimis trained on the occupants, then signaled for the others to enter.

POPOLOV LAY on the rubbing table, a towel over his rump, as Gregor massaged the muscles of his neck and back. The sweet smell of a fine perfumed oil permeated the room. The colonel held a telephone receiver to one ear.

"What the hell do you mean they're not there?" he shouted into the mouthpiece. "Where the hell are they?"

"Escaped. This place is demolished, Colonel. Not a piece of steel or wood standing. It's a miracle they got out alive," Obolensky reported.

"*How* did they get out?" Popolov shouted. "Where are they?" His face was flushed. Gregor had never seen him so angry.

"A trapdoor leads down to some rotted piers and a dock. Somehow they got out by boat."

"Where are they?"

"I don't know, Colonel. I've called in the army and put out a new bulletin. I can't get helicopters in the air tonight. It's too risky."

"I want this island blanketed with troops and helicopters. Don't talk to me of risks," Popolov said, still shouting. "Take the troops you have and start through the warehouses right now."

"I don't have enough men to start right now, Colonel."

"Where the hell are they?" Colonel Popolov screamed, his rage reaching the boiling point.

"Most of them are dead, Colonel."

Popolov slammed the receiver onto its cradle.

THE FARMHOUSE WAS a large two-story brick structure, dry and warm. The solemn middle-aged couple who ran the farm watched the foreigners who had taken over their home with looks of unconcealed hatred. Sanchez explained that they would not be hurt and that no more damage than necessary would be done, but it made no difference. Loyal party followers, they glared at the man with the huge mustache and turned from him.

Barrabas pulled Billy Two and O'Toole aside. "Our weapons situation isn't good," he said.

They didn't have to be told, and they nodded.

"Get something to eat and take the truck out. Find another vehicle for us and some guns. Try for some heavy stuff this time."

The SOBs waiting in the farmhouse settled down for the return of the forage party.

11

O'Toole and Billy Two had been given an almost impossible task, but they knew that the success of the mission depended on them. They had to find replacement weapons.

The truck they drove made them doubly vulnerable since it was sure to have been reported missing by now. They were both in Russian uniform, Billy in the one Nanos had worn earlier, although it was a couple of sizes too small.

"So where do we go?" Billy asked.

"Don't have a clue. The airport might have an arsenal, but we should stay clear of it for now," O'Toole offered. "I don't have any suggestions."

While they discussed the problem, headlights overtook them from the rear. They were on the coastal highway heading south past Tomari. The only weapons they had were the silenced Berettas they'd carried in their webbing when they'd landed. Each man transferred the handgun to a belt inside his Russian greatcoat.

An army truck pulled alongside and waved them over. O'Toole pulled over to the side and made sure Billy knew what his intentions were. "We get out, but stick to your own side of the truck—stay well apart. Count to three after I cough and go for your Beretta. At the worst, we'll get the first two who step out.''

"Got it."

O'Toole stepped from the truck, took two paces forward and stopped. The truck was between him and Billy. Two Russians got out of their vehicle, holding their AKs in combat position.

"We found this truck abandoned, Comrades. It was better than walking," O'Toole said, then coughed and cleared his throat.

Billy counted to three and rolled to his right, his hand going for the Beretta. O'Toole duplicated the maneuver on the left side of the truck. The AKs moved with them, and fingers tightened on the triggers. But the hands holding them were dead. Each Russian took two 9 mm slugs. Billy shot for the heart, O'Toole for the head. Their weapons were still aimed at the truck as the two bodies crumpled.

O'Toole waved Billy to cover him as he crawled to the back of the truck, stood to open the door and then jumped out of the line of fire.

Two rifles were tossed to the asphalt, and two kids in uniform stepped out, their hands in the air.

"Let's get out of here!" Billy shouted at Liam. "I'll hold these two in the back. Drive to a back road."

"Strip your comrades of all identification and put them in the front of our truck," O'Toole ordered the young Russians. He picked up the four AKs from the asphalt and climbed in the front of the army truck. Billy Two held his Beretta on the rookies, prodded them into the truck bed and motioned for them to lie on their bellies.

The army truck was ideal for the SOBs, big enough for ten in the back. O'Toole pulled onto a side road and five minutes later drove partway up a rutted farm road. He cut the lights. Suddenly it was very dark. The rain had stopped, but the sky was still overcast. He flipped on the dome light for the rear compartment and walked around to join Billy.

The two youngsters were scared. One of the soldiers was short, while the other, a farm kid who was probably as strong as an ox, was Billy's size.

"Tell him I want his uniform," Billy said.

They exchanged uniforms while O'Toole questioned the smaller one. He was about eighteen and was shaking uncontrollably.

"They've heard of us. Rumor has it we've killed hundreds of troops on the island. They think we're some kind of supermen."

"I believe that," Billy said. "They're only kids."

"How far is it to the closest military base?" O'Toole asked the short one in Russian.

"Close. Our training school is less than eight miles."

"What kind of armaments at the school?"

"Armaments?"

"Guns. You were carrying AKs. What else do you have?" O'Toole asked.

The taller of the two, who had been silent during the discussion, answered the question. "We have a place where they keep a lot of guns. A locked room."

"Is that where you came from, where this truck came from?" O'Toole asked.

Billy Two put his Beretta back in its webbing and pulled his commando knife. He held it to the neck of the tall kid and slid the blade along the skin, drawing blood.

"If you do not do exactly as I ask," O'Toole said to the short one, "my friend will slit your friend's throat. Now get up front with me and show me where this school is."

They drove for about six miles when O'Toole asked the prime question. "How many men at the school?"

"A hundred cadets. Ten instructors," the Russian answered, his lips trembling.

"When we get to the gate, you must act as if nothing is happening, unless you want your friend to die."

They pulled up to the gate. A veteran was training a recruit. He took one look at O'Toole, and without a word reached for a Makarov automatic in an outside holster.

O'Toole shot him through the head with his Beretta. It made little sound, but the effect was devastating. The back of the man's head hit the recruit and trickled down his face. The recruit put his hands to his face and opened his mouth to scream. O'Toole put a slug through the back of his mouth.

"Where do the instructors live?" O'Toole asked the young Russian captive.

"The rear... the rear of the compound."

O'Toole drove to the designated building and stopped the truck, turned off the ignition and turned to the youngster.

"You and your friend are going to live for only one reason. Propaganda. When your superiors find the school you must tell them what you've seen."

The youngster was too frightened to answer.

O'Toole dragged him from the cab and pushed him toward the truck and into the back. The two SOBs warriors locked the Russians in and then returned for the four AKs in the cab.

"That's the NCO barracks. Probably about eight or nine men in there. No noise, okay?"

Billy nodded. This was his show. He led the way inside and into a central corridor. Billy took the left side, O'Toole the right. In the first four rooms they checked, the officers were sleeping soundly.

O'Toole quietly closed a door and moved on to check the next room. He opened the door and walked right into the barrel of a Makarov automatic. The Russian pushed the barrel into his gut.

"What the hell's going on? What the hell are you?" he asked, his speech still slurred.

In the last few seconds he had on this earth, O'Toole heard a rush of blood from the next cubicle and a gargle of sound that could only be the arrival of death. He didn't hear the soft footsteps of his friend Billy, but the hairs bristling at the back of his neck told him the big man was there.

Suddenly a commando knife protruded from the man's forehead, buried to the hilt. O'Toole expected to hear the sound of an explosion and to feel his gut being ripped out, but it didn't come. As the Russian toppled to the bed, O'Toole grabbed the automatic from his hand and looked at the safety. It was still on.

He nodded to Billy as he moved past him and out the door. While Billy retrieved his prized knife, O'Toole found a bag and searched the building for weapons. He found eight Makarovs and at least a dozen clips of ammo. The Irishman wondered what these NCOs were doing with handguns usually used by the KGB.

Billy Two and O'Toole left the building and returned to the truck to question their two captives. "Where is the armory?" O'Toole asked the shorter Russian soldier.

The two men followed the youths to a small building at the rear of the compound. The door was locked. Billy kicked it in with one booted foot.

The place was almost empty. In one corner Styrofoam boxes were piled to the ceiling. Billy opened one. It contained a rifle, three magazines, an oil bottle, bayonet, tool kit, cotton sling and an instruction booklet.

"Ever seen one of these?" he asked O'Toole.

"I'll be damned. Where the hell did they get these?"

"What are they? Look like AKs, but a little different." Billy said.

"They're Chinese. Folding stock AK-56-1. An improvement on the Russian gun," O'Toole said.

Billy Two piled a half-dozen Styrofoam boxes on the tall Russian's outstretched arms. Then he moved to a pile of square crates against one wall and broke one open. "This is Brazilian stuff, Liam. Brazilian ammo," he said. "Must be a thousand rounds to each crate."

"Right. Twenty small boxes in each crate, fifty rounds to a box. We'll take one."

"Why the Chinese AKs and Brazilian ammo?" Billy wondered.

"Reliability. This is a training camp. They'll be issued Russian AKs and ammo when they're fully trained," Liam chuckled.

Billy had opened another crate and had a new rifle in his hand. "I know this one," he said. "Picked one off a dead Cambodian. It's Finnish and has the new plastic forearm."

"The select switch is awkward. Leave them. Take a few more boxes of the Chinese ones—they're less trouble," O'Toole said. He found a box of plastic explosive and some timers. He didn't need any more, but it gave him an idea. He rolled four pieces the size of sausages and attached the timers, handing them to the small Russian.

"Find any grenades?" he asked Billy.

"Just HE. How much?" the Osage asked.

"A hundred. One crate. Let's get out of here."

The four men moved outside to the truck. The Russian soldiers piled the crates of guns, ammo and grenades in the back.

"Stay with him, Billy. I'm taking the other one for a little walk." To the recruit he said in Russian, "Where's the communications room?"

Five minutes later they were back. "I set charges in the communications room and the main barracks," he told Billy.

"They're set for five minutes," he told the Russians. "If you can get to them and pull the timers from the plastique, you can save all your friends."

Billy Two and Liam O'Toole drove off in the Russian truck. When they reached the farm, the two mercs were greeted with enthusiasm. No merc is comfortable without a load of ammo at his side.

Barrabas looked over the weapons and had Hayes, Sanchez and Beck ready them for battle.

"Where did you get the Chinese stuff?" he asked.

"A long story, Colonel," O'Toole spoke for them. "A training school. Guess they needed reliable stuff. The 223s are Brazilian. Some of the best that are made."

"I noticed. Get some food and some sleep. The night isn't over yet."

He glanced at his watch. It was time to get the next show on the road.

12

The night was dark and wet. The mercs sat on the bench seat of the army truck as it made its way down the streets of Novikovo. Looking at the map, Barrabas realized they were only a few miles from where it all began, the beach off Mys Aniva where Moltsov met his death and their mission was almost aborted.

The VIP community was not large enough to make the search for Popolov's home impossible. Because they hadn't known how big Novikovo would be when they'd been at the farmhouse, the task had seemed impossible. But only a hundred odd houses made up the small village.

If he was as powerful as they had been told, only one home could belong to the notorious Colonel Popolov. It was the biggest one with two guards inside the gates and at least two patrolling the grounds. Sanchez parked the truck a block from the house. Barrabas unstrapped his backpack and pulled a package from under the few grenades that were left. He pulled out a passive night vision sight sealed in a plastic bag, and then slid open the window to the rear of the truck so that they could talk to O'Toole and Nanos.

"I've got an AN/PVS-4. I'm going to do a recon by myself," he told them. "We haven't got enough intelligence for a hard probe. They may have an army in there that we can't see."

He eased open the door of the truck, kept to the shadows and then hauled himself to the top of the wall surrounding the building. The wall had no sensors as far as he could tell. If there was sophisticated laser equipment on the corner posts of the wall or in the grounds, he wouldn't see them. The night vision sight would help him see in the dark, but it couldn't detect electronic sentries.

He scanned the grounds. Two men patrolled inside. The place kept no dogs, unless they were kenneled at the rear. No lights were on in the house. He left his perch and moved around the wall to the opposite side. He could only see two guards at the gate and two in the grounds. He scanned the grounds with the AN/PVS-4 and focused on every window, but came away with no more clues. Two things confirmed they had the right place: it was the only house in all of Novikovo with guards; and a black limousine, its military pennants fluttering in the night breeze, was parked in the driveway.

Back at the truck, Barrabas repacked the night sight while he told the others how it would go down. "The two guards inside the gates will have to be eliminated quickly. We don't want a signal from them to the house. Liam and Alex will take them out and assume their post. Nate, Billy Two and Hayes—you'd better discard your uniforms and go in like us. Lee, José and

I will take the other two guards and go inside. We'll come for you when we're finished.''

They waited for the two in back to change, then stole across the road, one at a time. They climbed the wall and regrouped behind a hedge.

''José and I will take out the guards in the grounds and secure the house,'' Barrabas told the group. ''We'll interrogate the guard before going in, otherwise it's a totally wet operation—knives outside, Berettas inside. Do not kill the colonel. Lee will check out the carriage house for a driver and domestics. Alex will circle back for the truck and drive it inside the grounds when the place is secured. If they have patrols from the local barracks, we don't want any loose ends.

''Okay. Let's move out,'' he concluded.

Five black figures snaked out in five directions. Nanos went straight for the closest guard at the gate while O'Toole circled around. When O'Toole signaled that he was in position, they came out of the night and with the flash of commando knives, severed the guards' jugulars as steel blades cut through to bone.

Sanchez caught his man alone. He crawled to within five feet, jumped on the man's back, pulled his chin back and wiped the sharp blade through unresisting flesh until only a soft choking of blood pouring into lungs disturbed the night.

Barrabas had the toughest job. He had to knock the guard unconscious and drag him to the bushes in the shadows away from the house. He used the butt of his

Beretta to bring the man down, hitting him hard enough to stun, but not to put him away for hours.

Hatton sneaked up to the limousine and made a full circle of the carriage house before making her decision. The lower half was a garage containing two antique sports cars. That explained why the limo was outside but didn't explain Russian decadence.

Barrabas and Sanchez crossed the lawn from the shadows next to the wall. Barrabas motioned to her and led the way to the front door.

"Popolov is in a back bedroom on the second floor," Barrabas said. "A servant occupies part of the top floor. Every corner of this place is wired for TV scanning. The monitors are all in a third-floor room." He repeated all he'd learned from the guard before the man died. "Two domestics, military trained, also sleep on the third floor. We try to keep Popolov and his servant alive. I go for Popolov. Lee, you and Sanchez take out the man, bring him to Popolov's bedroom and make sure all of his surveillance equipment is out of commission. Let's go."

Inside the house, they made a quick survey of the ground floor and found no one. They crept silently to the second-floor bedroom. Barrabas disappeared inside, while Hatton and Sanchez moved silently to the third floor.

Together they moved from room to room until they found their target. Sanchez left Hatton at the servant's door and checked the remaining rooms. All were empty. When he returned to the Russian's door, Lee Hatton was sitting calmly in a comfortable chair, her gun trained on the servant, while he pleaded for his life in perfect Oxford English.

"Does Colonel Popolov speak English?" she asked as Sanchez entered.

"He will tell you not, but he was trained at the Lumumba School in Moscow with many Westerners. He learned from them." The man was sitting up in bed, his hands raised, with two bullet holes in the wall behind him, each about an inch from his ears.

Sanchez grinned. He was really beginning to like this woman. He had been a loner all his life. If he had one like her for himself, he might consider some kind of union. But he knew Hatton was not for him, and sadly he realized he'd probably never find one like her again.

"Let's get him downstairs to Barrabas," Sanchez suggested. "Unless you have some more questions."

"No," she said, getting to her feet, waving the Russian to the door with the Beretta.

They walked down the stairs, Sanchez in front, their captive and then Hatton bringing up the rear. Sanchez had his Beretta in hand, not taking anything for granted.

They moved into Popolov's room in single file to hear the irate colonel shouting at Barrabas who, like Hatton before him, was sitting in a comfortable chair pointing his Beretta 93-R at the livid Russian.

Popolov was sitting up in a huge canopy bed on a raised dais. A huge grin on his face, Barrabas sat to one side with a clear shot to the bed and his back to the wall.

"He speaks English, Colonel," Sanchez said. Then he turned to Popolov and in Russian said, "Might as well humor the man, Popolov. He's going to kill you if you don't."

"You are the one who was brought in by Moltsov?" the Russian asked.

"The same."

"You won't last for more than a few hours if you kill me. Every man on the island will be after you." The cornered Russian spit it out through clenched teeth.

"Sorry, Popolov. It won't work. We've been here for more than twenty-four hours with every one of your men after us, and yet here we are. Your guards are all dead. Your communications are out. And you are a marked man."

"I'd like to work on this one first," Lee said, pointing to the servant.

"You're the doctor," Barrabas replied.

Sanchez muscled the small man to a divan in a corner of the massive bedroom.

"I'll use Pentothal on him first," she said, as if to herself. "Although the combination of Pentothal and scopolamine might kill him."

The servant's eyes rolled up into their sockets as Sanchez held him while Hatton injected the serum. "We will wait a few minutes," she said as her victim calmed and lay still.

"Go down and see how our people are," Barrabas told Sanchez. "We'll handle this for now. Report back if you are not needed there."

"The English may not come out under the drugs, Colonel. We may need José," Lee Hatton said.

Popolov was looking at Hatton with undisguised hatred. Barrabas couldn't figure out if it was because she was handling the needles or because she was a woman. He could see the Russian was a worried man who had a lot to lose.

"What are your duties here?" Hatton asked her patient.

The answer came clearly enough, but the voice was without emotion. "I am Colonel Popolov's personal servant. I run his house, monitor the rooms, record the activities of visitors."

"What kind of visitors?"

"VIPs from Moscow, subordinates, the women."

"And what do you record?"

"Conversations between Colonel Popolov and his guests, everything that goes on in the house."

"Is this on video?"

"Yes."

Hatton was feeling her way, taking her time. Barrabas looked at his Rolex. "It's almost five, Lee. Let's not take any more time than necessary," he said.

Alarmed, the Russian colonel sat up straight. "Lee?" he asked. "Lee Hatton?"

Hatton and Barrabas didn't answer. The contortions of visible hatred warped the colonel's face as he looked at Lee. "You are the one!" He pointed an accusing finger. "You defeated my cousin!"

"That explains a lot," Barrabas said. He turned to Hatton. "Go ahead, Lee."

With the clue from the Russian colonel, she continued. "What does Colonel Popolov fear most in life?"

The prostrate servant squirmed, fighting the drug, but finally, in a voice tinged with fear, he answered, "The Room. Pain."

"Tell me about 'the Room.' What is special about it?" she asked.

The man squirmed, compressed his lips and refused to answer, no matter what she did. She reached for the second needle, found a vein and plunged it home. He could not resist the combination of the two drugs. She pulled a stethoscope from beneath her jump suit and listened to his heartbeat. It was rapid. After a few seconds, she asked again.

"Tell me about the Room."

Sanchez came in as they waited for the answer. He was about to talk. Barrabas waved him to silence.

"I can't talk about the Room! I hate the Room!"

The pitiful man's head thrashed from side to side. He convulsed once and lay still. Doc Lee sounded his chest, looked up and shook her head.

Barrabas looked at Sanchez, then nodded.

"They're okay, Colonel. Nanos brought the truck in. They used the greatcoats they had before. The others were covered in blood."

"Take a look in the basement. We should have covered it when he came in," Barrabas said.

Barrabas stood, ripped a sash cord from a window, cut it in half with his commando knife and tied the Russian colonel's limbs together.

Lee moved over from the divan and opened her case again. She withdrew two syringes, depressed one plunger to clear the needle of air, and quickly injected the Russian in one arm.

After only a moment of delay, she asked her first question. "Who ordered the KAL flight shot down?"

The answer came without hesitation. But it was in Russian.

They didn't understand.

"How long before he will come around?" Barrabas asked.

"At least an hour. I didn't bring anything to speed it up."

"We'll have to wait for Sanchez," Barrabas said. As if on cue, Sanchez returned at that moment. "Colonel, I checked out the cellars. There's an interrogation room. And a lot of sophisticated modern devices for getting answers out of reluctant prisoners."

Barrabas nodded slowly. He turned to Dr. Hatton.

"Do you think he might talk even more if we took him to the scene of his own crimes?"

Lee thought for a moment. "Might be worth a try."

"Let's do it." He pulled his knife, cut the bonds and hefted the man onto his back.

Hatton put away her instruments and stepped briskly into the hall. Barrabas and Sanchez lugged the heavy colonel and fell in behind her. In a procession along the dimly lit corridors they followed the doctor to the first floor and down a wide stone stairway to the basement.

Lights burned brightly below ground level where Sanchez had turned them on during his first visit. He indicated an open door leading into a square room even brighter than the hall.

They stood still, riveted by the sight.

The devices were familiar to intelligence agencies and military dictatorships the world over. Several wooden chairs were wrapped in electric wires that could be attached to the genitals, tongues, scalp, fingers and nipples. Wires led to a black box on a disk that controlled the electric current.

Nearby was a padded rack with leather straps like a doctor's examination gurney. On an adjacent table were wooden paddles and hard rubber batons, the kind that could cripple and maim with a minimum of external bruising. The concrete floor had been stained with blood.

Barrabas shrugged off the weight of the man on his back and dropped him to the floor. Popolov whimpered with fear, his eyes glazed from the effects of the drugs and the dawning realization of where he was.

Barrabas prodded him with a hard boot. The Russian screamed.

"Speak to me in English," Barrabas demanded.

Popolov howled. "Don't hurt me. I can't stand it!"

Barrabas leaned close to his ear, whispering his questions.

"Who ordered the Korean jet shot down. And why?"

"I did. Orders from Moscow," Popolov said.

Barrabas gripped the man in a rage, his biceps bulging. He hefted the man up and threw him into one of the interrogation chairs.

"Talk, Popolov! Or we hook you up and start frying!"

"No! No! I'll tell you anything. Anything! I have a plot under way. In six weeks, the Spetsnaz will go into Afghanistan to kidnap the rebel leaders." Spittle from his mouth dripped down his chin. "Without their leaders," he went on haltingly, "the Afghans will be helpless, and we can concentrate on moving into Pakistan."

"Why are you so motivated by this mission? What is your personal gain to be?"

"General Persof is an enemy of the KGB within the Presidium. I have fed the plot to him through his son. The general will take over, and my cousin's force will come under his command."

"Balandin?"

"My cousin."

"What's the catch, Popolov? Why let Persof take the credit?"

The answer was long in coming, but when it came, it was clear enough and believable.

"It will not be to his credit. If he is successful, the Americans will have to step in, and we'll finally lose Afghanistan. If he fails, then I win."

Barrabas walked from the table, waving the other two to the hallway. "What do you think? Is this for real?"

"I think so," Hatton said. "It's too farfetched for him to dream up."

"Now, think about the Korean jet," Barrabas whispered in Popolov's ear when he returned to the main room. "If you come up with the answer I want, I'm finished with you."

Barrabas turned to Sanchez and Hatton and spoke quietly. "Did you destroy all of the monitoring equipment in the house?" he asked.

"All the connectors to the distribution system," Sanchez said.

"Think you can find a camera that works? We need a camera, videotape recorder and a monitor."

"Can do."

"Set it up in Popolov's bedroom. Make sure we've got a fresh tape. We'll bring him up."

Barrabas looked at his watch. It was almost six. They had less than an hour till sunrise.

"Who ordered you to shoot down the civilian jet? This is your last chance."

"Anthony Jones Hopkins."

Barrabas and Hatton looked each other, puzzled.

"Explain," Barrabas ordered.

"Hopkins is working for us."

"But why the Korean jet?" Barrabas asked, his tone showing his shock at Popolov's disclosure. Anthony Jones Hopkins was the assistant director of the CIA. He was being touted as the organization's next director.

"We tried in 1978, but no one was killed. Diplomatic notes were exchanged." The Russian could not speak clearly, but Barrabas was not going to let up on him now.

"What was the purpose?"

"War. A few hawks in the Pentagon—some in government—and Hopkins and a half-dozen in the CIA. The President is always too weak. Someone had to move the aggression ahead."

"But *why*?" Lee Hatton screamed from her place behind the table.

Barrabas looked at Hatton and saw tears in her eyes for the first time since he'd known her. It was sick, but it was true. People in democratic governments had done it before. Hopkins could be a deep plant of the Soviets. It was the kind of mixed up philosophy not uncommon within the struggle for world power.

Barrabas took Popolov through a partial list of the Americans involved and reviewed the Afghanistan plot again. Just as he finished, Sanchez returned.

"It's all set up in the bedroom," Sanchez told Barrabas.

"Thanks. Wait outside with O'Toole and Nanos."

Barrabas turned to Hatton. "This has to stop right here with you and me. I give it to Jessup, then we forget it."

"It's monstrous. Do we really have people like that in our government?" she asked.

"Yes. It's a closed issue, Lee. Got that?"

She held her head in her hands, then looked up. "I wish I didn't know, but since I do, I'll keep it to myself. What are you going to do now?"

"Dress him in his best uniform. He's going to become a television star."

"Are we like him, Nile? Are we monsters traveling from place to place exerting the will of our people at the end of a gun barrel?" she asked.

"If you don't know the answer to that, Lee, you'd better take a long vacation."

"It's just—"

"I know. It's unreal. Take it from me, we're not like the Popolovs and the Balandins of this world."

They took Popolov, who was little more than a zombie, upstairs to his own bedroom. They dressed him and put him in front of the camera. The atmosphere of his bedroom, the feel of his uniform—his sign of authority—brought him around somewhat. He answered all of Barrabas's questions with flair. The tape would be totally believable.

Barrabas turned off the machine, handed the tape to Lee and asked her to wait for him downstairs. When she had gone, he looked at the madman sitting erect in front of the dead camera, still smiling as if facing his admirers.

Suddenly, like a wave washing over him, Popolov's eyes changed, the expression of simple arrogance replaced by savagery. Barrabas recognized it—the look of a tamed animal gone wild.

The Russian threw himself forward, his hands digging into Barrabas's neck like steel claws. The American teetered backward, caught off-balance by Popolov's bulk and the surprise attack. He fished wildly for his Beretta, pulling it from his belt and jamming it against the madman's temple.

He squeezed.

The impact was almost silent. Popolov's eyes froze as his brains slid out the other side of his head. His grip relaxed, and he sank heavily to the floor.

13

It was almost dawn when Barrabas and Hatton walked from the house. They were subdued and anxious to get out of the foul atmosphere of the place. Sanchez had told Nanos and O'Toole about the gruesome cellar.

"Give me a few minutes in the house, Colonel," O'Toole said.

Barrabas nodded absently. "Get the limousine started, Alex. We'll use it for cover until we get into the mountains."

O'Toole was out of the house in minutes, and the limo was standing next to the truck, both idling. Nanos had found a supply of gas in the garage and had filled both tanks.

"José will drive the limo with Alex in back," Barrabas said. "Liam will drive the truck with Lee and me in back." He turned to Sanchez. "Drive all the way up to Makarov and don't stop for anything. We'll follow in convoy. No one is going to question Popolov's car."

"What then?" Sanchez asked.

Barrabas looked at his watch. "It will soon be 0700. We won't be at Makarov until almost 0900," he said. "We'll pick a side road heading north and abandon the limo, then take the truck south to the farm."

"The charges are set to go in one hour," O'Toole said. "Is that going to screw up your plan?"

"Let's hope not, Liam. They could have an early morning guard change, and that would also spoil our plan. If we're stopped, José will do the talking. They'll barely see Alex through the dark glass."

He looked from one to the other. They all looked weary, especially Lee. "Okay," he said. "Let's get out of here."

The convoy moved through Novikovo and up the coast road. They bypassed Yuzhno-Sakhalinsk and drove majestically through Dolinsk with pennants flying. Every military man they passed saluted the car.

By eight they were more than halfway to Makarov and had encountered no resistance. O'Toole's charges would have blown by then. Word would soon be out to stop the limo. If they stopped now, they would be too close to the farm.

At 0830, they were on the southern outskirts of Makarov.

"Pass the car and lead them inland away from the coast road," he ordered O'Toole.

The convoy turned west and through a maze of streets not far from the computer center. At the dead end of one street, they stopped, left a charge in the limo set for ten minutes, and then drove north.

"Go past the computer center," Barrabas ordered Sanchez. "I want to see if they've changed the security."

The computer building was as they'd left it, except for the guard. Four guards patrolled the front of the building and two the back. They didn't seem too concerned that the enemy would strike there again.

"Okay. Let's head for the farm," Barrabas said. It had been a long and tough night.

MAJOR GAVRILL OBOLENSKY STOOD with a dozen of his KGB agents inside the gates of Popolov's home and watched the pitiful attempts of the military fire brigade to control the fire. He had put out a call to intercept Popolov's limousine, but felt that the enemy would have been smart enough to dump it by now.

His emotions were running high. He was a dedicated agent of the state. To know that his superior officer had been killed by enemy infiltration angered him. But the death of the monster he worked for was not a source of pain. He envied the man his riches and felt guilty about an emotion that was foreign to him. No matter. The island would have a new KGB chief, and Colonel Nekrasov would assume the military command that was rightfully his.

FROM A NEARBY OBSERVATION POINT, Lieutenant Anatole Persof watched the firefighters' vain efforts to quell the raging blaze. His emotions were mixed. He had told his father about the Afghanistan plot. His father had been pleased with his work, praised him as he never had before. He had hoped to pump Popolov further for information to pass on to his father, who, until now, had looked on him as weak and helpless.

His father hated Popolov with a passion. He was a member of the Presidium and was violently opposed to the constant lobbying and political intrigue of his enemy, Ladislav Buruka, the head of the KGB. He would do anything to weaken the man's position, convinced it was for the good of the state.

His father had jumped at the chance to take over the Afghanistan plot, and Popolov's death wouldn't change that. The older Persof had encouraged his son to undermine Popolov at every opportunity. He had told his son that the man was a menace, unbalanced, and could only do the state irreparable harm. Young Persof had come away from the conversation convinced he should work for his father from inside Popolov's organization.

Now it was too late for his dreams of glory. Someone else had gotten to Popolov and had gone further than Persof would ever have gone. It was too late.

As he stood on the fringe of the action, he had a flash of insight and knew it wasn't too late for him. It was just the beginning. He would tell his father that he had used the infiltration of the island as a blind. He, not the invaders, had destroyed his father's enemy. He, Persof, had followed his father's orders.

He would ask one favor. A transfer to Balandin's Spetsnaz to be their political adviser, the watchdog of the KGB. His father could swing it. He would write to Balandin, tell him he was the last to see Popolov alive and that they had started to be great friends.

It was time for Anatole Persof to break out of the mold.

NILE BARRABAS SAT in the back of the truck with Lee Hatton as the SOBs left Makarov. Sanchez and

O'Toole were in front. Nanos had his head partway through the partition talking to the men up front.

"We've been through some bad ones, but this mission bothers me most," Lee said.

"You want to shut it out of your head, but it just won't go away," he said. "All we can do is give it to Jessup and trust that he knows how to handle it. Cleaning up Washington's backyard is not our specialty."

"It stinks.

"What are you going to do about the computer building?" she asked.

"I honestly don't know. I'm so pissed off with the Soviets right now that I'd like to destroy the whole island. But those tapes have to get out of here."

As they turned onto the farm road, an olive-green army ambulance came careering at them at full speed, its flasher sending out bright splashes of light. Sanchez turned hard to the right, and his passengers were thrown to the side of the truck. Immediately they were all out and in a defensive position, their AK-47s leveled at the ambulance that had stopped across the road. Its personnel had piled out and were in the grass beside the road, their machine guns raised.

Barrabas stuck his head up a few inches and was met with a hail of bullets from the other side. But he had seen enough.

He turned to O'Toole. "Will you tell Billy Two to stop firing at me?" he asked.

O'Toole grinned and shouted across the road. They all—including Billy Two, Hayes and Beck who had been at the farm—met on the crest of the muddy road, happy to be reunited.

"We've got to get out of here, Colonel," Billy Two said. "The farmer got away from us and set fire to the barn."

"How the hell did you get an army ambulance?" Barrabas asked.

"Nate was bored. He hijacked it from a couple of AWOL medics who came our way."

Barrabas could see the smoke from the fire and knew someone would be along soon. He looked around. "Let's get out of here. You follow our truck. We'll find a better place to park."

Barrabas sat up front with Sanchez. Nanos drove the ambulance. The others were in the back of the truck. All the arms had been saved and were stashed in the back of the ambulance.

They drove to the west coast highway and headed north. Barrabas decided to move into territory where they'd never been seen.

They took side roads to bypass Uglegorsk and stopped on a dead-end road off a mountain trail inland from Boshnyakov. "Is your Russian good enough to examine Russian identification?" Barrabas asked Sanchez.

"I think so. I spent a lot of time in southern Russia, the Georgian provinces. My accent is not Muscovite, but I can get by. What have you got in mind, Colonel?"

"A roadblock. We set up our own roadblock."

Barrabas could see the wicked grin on Billy's face. This was the kind of thinking he liked. None of the mercs were meant to hide and skulk around.

"We drive the coast road and see how the Russians have set up their roadblocks and pick our spot."

"I like it," Sanchez said, pulling the truck back toward the highway.

LADISLOV BURUKA SAT in a massive chair behind an equally massive desk in a huge room on the top floor of a granite structure overlooking Dzerzhinsky Square, home of the dreaded Komitet Gosudarstvennoi Bezopasnosti, the KGB.

The room was plain, as befitted the peasant character of the man who had risen to such an exalted rank. But it was also rich. The wood paneling had been stripped from the libraries of three Georgian mansions, homes of men he had sent to the Gulag. The priceless paintings, hung with such care, had been smuggled from hidden caches the Germans had secreted into what was now East Germany. Buruka was a man of simple taste as long as it was exclusive and expensive. His organization was the same. Simple tactics worked better than elaborate ones.

Buruka's only indulgence had concerned his friend Popolov, the man whom he had once groomed to fill his shoes, but who had lately served only as an alter ego—a man who performed as he himself would like to, but could not.

Now Popolov was dead.

The man of power clipped the end off a Havana cigar. He lit it from an expensive lighter presented to him by the premier himself. He sat in the huge chair and blew smoke rings toward the ceiling.

Popolov was dead. Somehow the island had been infiltrated. Popolov had not been able to handle it. He had called Major Obolensky and put him in charge temporarily. He had no faith in the ability of the bungling Colonel Nekrasov and had already called General Persof to request that the man be relieved.

One didn't tell Persof anything, one merely requested. Some day he would get something on Persof and end his career. The general had a son on Sakhalin. He was with the KGB. Maybe something could be arranged. Maybe he could be transferred to hazardous duty somewhere.

Buruka loved power. He loved his little intrigues and the moving of pawns on the board. Young Persof could become a pawn to make his father bend. He would give it some thought.

AT THEIR ROADBLOCK just north of Uglegorsk, the SOBs were enjoying themselves immensely. In the rural setting, they had room to maneuver. An old building on the shoreline was not right for them as a hideout, but it was ideal to stash vehicles and supplies.

They now had a second truck to complement the first. The ambulance was at the back of the old building. Billy Two and O'Toole had become restless and set out alone in a captured army staff car. They were looking for a hideaway, food and medical supplies. Operating with few supplies was not new to the SOBs.

Foraging was as much a part of their action as it had been for armies in centuries past.

Barrabas manned the barricade with Sanchez, Nanos, Beck and Hayes. By now they all wore army uniforms but kept their own battle clothes underneath. The temperature on Sakhalin never seemed to move above forty-five degrees, so the extra clothes were no problem.

Hayes and Beck were positioned in ditches on the sides of the road. Barrabas sat in an army vehicle, dressed in an officer's uniform. He, Beck and Hayes had their Chinese AK-56-1s trained on the road.

Some vehicles Sanchez allowed to pass. Others he ordered emptied. The prisoners were bound and gagged inside the warehouse. Weapons and ammunition were quickly stockpiled.

Barrabas began to be concerned. It was almost noon. Someone would be asking questions about the missing men and vehicles soon. When Billy Two and Liam returned, they would have to move on.

Suddenly an armored troop carrier came into view. It would be at the barricade soon. The SOBs had some rocket grenade launchers and a case of the grenades stashed behind the old building, but hadn't been prepared for an armored assault here. Hayes and Beck crept closer, reached underneath their Russian greatcoats to their webbing and each unclipped two grenades. It was the best they could do under the circumstances.

Sanchez walked to the front of the barricade as usual, holding out one hand. Barrabas had to credit his new man. He had proved invaluable to them on this trip.

The armored vehicle stopped thirty feet from the barricade. A 40 mm machine gun traversed, then came to rest pointing at Sanchez's chest. Hayes and Beck tensed, ready for action.

The hatch opened. A head covered with flaming red hair emerged. "What do you think of this baby, Colonel?" O'Toole shouted.

Hayes and Beck emerged from the ditch. Sanchez and Nanos walked closer. Barrabas wasn't amused.

"Let's get these vehicles behind the building," he shouted. "Move it!"

They had a motor pool to choose from and moved off with every military man on the island looking for them. A new four-wheel drive staff car led the parade with Sanchez driving and Barrabas lounging in back in his officer's uniform. The armored personnel carrier was next in line with Nanos driving. O'Toole drove a covered truck with Billy Two and Beck sitting on the tailgate, their AKs on their laps as they'd seen Russian troopers sit. They didn't need the cavalcade, but it looked more impressive this way.

Billy Two and O'Toole had found an empty truck repair shop two blocks from the computer center at Makarov. One man lived in the back. The place had obviously not serviced a truck in years.

The SOBs drove in and, by 1400 hours they had secured their position, set up a watch two hours apart, and sat down to a well-deserved meal.

With a chipped mug in hand, the steam from black coffee curling over his lips, Barrabas walked to a corner to finish his coffee and make a decision. The garage was large. He couldn't see all his people from where he stood. Billy Two was sitting on the hood of an old wreck in the opposite corner, talking to Nanos. They laughed about something. It was good that they could still laugh, Barrabas thought to himself.

Should they make a try for the computer center, which was so vulnerable and so close by? If they tried and died in the attempt, they might destroy all Russian storage of vital military data and do massive damage to Russian research for years to come. But America would never have the proof needed to clear the air on the Korean crash. Americans would never know about the traitors at high levels in their own ranks.

If Jessup was there, he'd say "To hell with the computer center. Get the bloody tapes home." But Jessup wasn't there. It was up to Barrabas. Get them out with what they had or go for broke. It was up to him, the burden of command and the liability of patriotism.

Lastly, he had to think about his people. They were being paid to learn about the Korean incident, and they'd already done that and more. Christ, the fact they'd done what they had on this fortress of an island was a military miracle.

It was 1800 hours and starting to get dark. If they didn't get out tonight, they never would.

14

On the west coast road south of Boshnyakov, Major Obolensky and Colonel Nekrasov stood at the spot where the SOBs had operated their roadblock.

"We are always a few hours behind those bastards," Nekrasov said, shaking his head. "The last time, it cost Popolov his life."

"Let's not be hypocrites, Colonel. Their work at Novikovo is the only good thing that's come of this," Obolensky said with an impish grin on his face. Obolensky was a career KGB man, but he had an uncommon sense of humor and a "feel" for people.

Nekrasov looked up and down the road. It was past 1600 hours and dark. The heavy cloud cover of the past few days had lifted, allowing a few stars to peek through the remaining clouds that drifted intermittently across the sky. It was still cool. Both men were dressed warmly. Nekrasov looked over at the old building the SOBs had used as a screen.

"Show me the rest of it," the colonel said.

They walked the two hundred yards to the scene of carnage. The abandoned ambulance stood alone. Four other vehicles had been left demolished by the SOBs.

"How many men were overcome this time?" Nekrasov asked, his tone betraying his foul mood.

"Fifteen."

"How could they do it, Gavrill? How could they do it so cleanly?"

Obolensky had never heard Colonel Nekrasov use his first name and hadn't realized he even knew it. "Traffic is light here, Colonel. We have hundreds of roadblocks set up all over the island," he said. "Actually, it was a brilliant move. They stripped our people of their arms. We count scores of automatic rifles missing, three antitank grenade launchers, a 40 mm machine gun. The list goes on."

He stopped to take a cigarette case out of his pocket and offered one to Nekrasov. They turned their backs to the wind, hunching together to light up.

"I was at Makarov when our people shredded the warehouse to eliminate them. Still can't figure how they got to the boat under that hail of fire," Obolensky said.

"However they did it, we've got to stop them, Major. Our reputations in Moscow are suspect already. We've got to eliminate them and do it fast."

They were walking back to the highway and to their cars. Neither man had slept more than a few hours in the past thirty-six. They had seen the beach at Mys Aniva, the farmhouse up the coast from Mys Krilon, the warehouse at Makarov and the devastation at Popolov's Novikovo home.

"What are they after?" Obolensky asked, as much to himself as to Nekrasov. "They raided our central computer storage. They interrogated Popolov and his man Gregor. Surely they have what they came for by now."

"Let's hope they don't have what they came for, Major. If they do, then they have probably gone. If not, they are looking for a way out."

"We have patrol boats circling the island, spotter planes crisscrossing every square mile. We've doubled the guard on all airports. The next move is up to them, Colonel."

"The next move has been up to them since Moltsov confessed their coming, Major. And we have been one step behind. I suggest we catch up quickly, or you and I will find ourselves in Moscow, trying to explain the unexplainable."

"All right. If they are still here, they are holed up somewhere. I'd like to know two things," Obolensky said. "Where are they and do they have another target?"

"Our count shows they have three vehicles—one an armored personnel carrier. If they have gone underground, it would have to be more than a farmhouse," Nekrasov said. "They will be in a large enough building to house three vehicles. I suggest we scour the island for such a place."

Obolensky lit another cigarette from the first. He was going over in his mind what they might be after. Finally he voiced what had been bothering him. "What the hell are they after?"

"What are they after?" Nekrasov repeated. "You and I have been entrusted with the finest fighting men and equipment in the Soviet Union. They could hijack one of our Foxhounds. The Americans have wanted to get a good look at one for the past year. They could be after one of our nuclear subs. It could be one of a half-dozen targets."

"One we can rule out," Obolensky said. "They have hit the computer center. They were there long enough to get whatever they were looking for. We don't have to worry about that."

"I agree. I also feel they will be holed up close to their next target. We'll concentrate our search close to the coastal targets at Poronaysk, Vakhrushev and Bykov where our naval forces are concentrated," the colonel said, reaching for his own cigarettes.

"And all military airports," Obolensky suggested. "A military jet would be the perfect escape route. We must triple our guard."

"That should do it, Major," Nekrasov said as he climbed into his staff car. "I have an emergency base set up at the capital. If you need me, call me there."

Obolensky watched the new staff car pull away and shifted his thoughts back to the invaders. Were there only ten? What were they after? How would they try to get out? The questions had been haunting him, and he wasn't coming up with the answers. If he didn't come up with the answers soon—if they got away from him, from this bastion of Soviet strength—it would be a blow to Soviet prestige and it would end his career, perhaps his life.

NOT TEN MILES AWAY AT MAKAROV, Nile Barrabas looked around the garage. They'd been there for only four hours, but he had itchy feet to get out. His people relaxed, taking an hour of sleep.

He had to wake them. He felt they would be found if they stayed put too long. It was almost midnight. Time for them to move. He walked up to where O'Toole and Billy Two were curled up in the bed of an old truck.

"Liam." Barrabas shook the redhead until he opened sleep-starved eyes.

"Colonel?"

"Time to talk over our next move. Get them rounded up, Liam, and bring them to the far end of the garage."

In minutes, Barrabas and the SOBs sat in a circle on the flatbed of an old wreck of a truck.

"I've been trying to decide whether to destroy the computer center or just make a run for it."

"What's the plan, Colonel?" O'Toole asked.

"You are being paid to find out who ordered the Korean jet shot down, and we've got that. We've got so much more than we came for that Jessup and his people should be forever grateful."

"So what's the problem, Colonel?" Billy Two asked.

"The problem is the computer center." Barrabas looked around the circle of faces. They had gone through hell in the past two days. But they were professionals. Christ, they were the best! He didn't want to ask them to risk more. "It contains probably every scientific development they have," he went on. "The scientist Fedesoff said they have no backup. That means if we destroy it—all the tapes—we could set the Soviets back ten years." He paused, looking around the circle.

"I repeat Billy's question," Beck said. "What's the problem, Colonel?"

"Okay. It's a risk. Not just our lives. We have information already that's incredible. Not just what you got from the computer center, Nate. We got something out of Popolov that will shake the foundations of Washington."

"Shit, Colonel!" Sanchez said. "If it's that big, we can't risk it. But why can't we split up?"

"Explain."

"We can't leave the computer center as it is, right? So four or five of us go after it, and the others get the hell out of here while we create the diversion," the new man suggested.

"Could work," Barrabas said. "Let's develop the thought. Sanchez is the only one who can fly us out. If we split and he can fly, only half of us get out."

"So we set it up so someone takes him to the plane and we have a timetable," Nanos offered. "If the computer force doesn't get to the airport at a set time, the Sanchez group takes off with the tapes we have."

"You all know that we don't have to do this," Barrabas reminded them. "It's not part of the official job. So let's vote." He raised his arm.

They all looked at him without expression, and one by one each raised a hand. It was a touching sight. Six hardened warriors deep in the heart of the strongest fortress the enemy possessed, all voting to give the enemy more hell than they could handle, even knowing they could die in the attempt.

"Someone mentioned a diversion," Barrabas said, starting into the plan they'd agreed to attempt. "We may have to have three forces. One to get Sanchez to an aircraft with the tapes, one to attack the computer center, one to create diversions so they won't send their whole army to the computer center."

"The best diversion would be a series of explosions all over Makarov and anywhere else we can reach," said O'Toole, the demolitions expert.

"We've got enough C-4 plastique and timers to accomplish that. But if we use it, we can't blow the computer center," Beck said. "Explosives might not destroy all the tapes, anyway. What we need are a few hundred phosphorus grenades."

"You're the resident genius in computers, Nate," Barrabas said. "What else will destroy magnetic tapes?"

"I don't get you, Colonel."

"Your head is so stuffed with the software and the console that you're forgetting the basics," Barrabas said with an enigmatic smile on his face.

Nate Beck looked puzzled.

"Magnets, Nate. The lowliest operator knows to keep his tapes and disks away from magnets."

"So?" Nate was still puzzled.

"What do you think those cranes in the scrapyard across the street from the computer center are?" Barrabas asked with a grin creasing his face.

"Magnets! You goddamned genius!" Beck shouted, unable to contain his enthusiasm. "The biggest fucking magnets on the island. Shit! If they can move scrap around that yard, they'll wipe every tape in the whole building in no time."

"First, Lee is the best qualified to make sure Sanchez gets to the airport with the tapes. It won't be easy. You'll have to overcome all the guards at the airport and have a plane ready for our arrival." He looked at Lee who nodded in return.

"We're talking Il'inskiy," Barrabas went on. "It's civilian, so it won't be as well guarded. When we went past, I noticed a few jets. Okay?" He looked at his watch. It was 0100 hours. "We have to be finished at 0400. I have two minutes after 0100." He looked at the others. They checked their watches and waited for orders.

"Liam is the best explosives man we have. He's going to create our diversions," Barrabas said. "This is an open order, Liam. Take all the C-4 you can carry. Start with military installations around Makarov to draw them away from us. Change vehicles frequently. Hit them up and down both coasts. Work your way back to Makarov for your last few charges and make your way to the airport by 0400. We won't wait for one minute."

O'Toole nodded. He knew he was the best for the job and would get a kick out of doing it. Not just the demolition, but the hares and hounds bit. There was nothing he liked better than confusing the enemy while they searched for one elusive bomber.

"That leaves Nate, Claude, Billy Two, Alex and I," Barrabas said. "I know Nate can handle a crane. Who else has experience?" he asked.

"I've handled lots of heavy equipment," Nanos said smiling. "I'm your man."

"We're talking cranes, Alex. Not dames," Hayes said, laughing.

"All right, guys. That leaves Billy Two, Claude and me to defend the crane operators," Barrabas said. "I'd feel better if we had three armored vehicles instead of one."

"If we had time, Billy and I could pick up a couple more," O'Toole said.

"How much risk?" Barrabas asked.

"Minimum. We take one of the trucks and bring back two armored cars. A half hour. That leaves us two for the computer center."

"All right. We'll do it," Barrabas said. "Make sure there's something heavy mounted on them—something like the 40 mm we have on the one we've got." He turned to the others. "While they get the armor, Beck and Nanos will check over the cranes. Make sure they're in good working order. We'd be in bad shape if they didn't work when the time came. Any questions?" he asked.

The circle of soldiers had nothing to say. They had the look of anticipation on their faces that Barrabas always felt when he was going into a good fight, one he had planned and could control—within limits.

"All right," he said. "Let's do it. Be back here at 0200."

Within two minutes, the trucks were started; Barrabas watched them leave—the sound of their departure fading within seconds. They were good men. The best. In the silence, the three men and one woman who remained stood for a moment, each with his own private thoughts, then Hayes and Sanchez broke off for an hour of sleep.

"I don't much care for this place, Colonel," Lee said. "With what we've learned, we should get the hell out of here."

"Give it a couple of hours, Lee, and we'll put this place behind us," he told her.

Barrabas jumped off the back of the troop carrier and made his way to a far corner and an old cot. With bloodshot eyes he looked at the Rolex that Erika had given him and set it to signal him in twenty minutes. In less than ten seconds he was asleep.

15

By 0200 hours the sky had again clouded over. A yellow half moon that had brightened the harsh landscape of Sakhalin for a few hours was hidden again. A brisk wind blew in from the Sea of Okhotsk, bending maple and pine trees.

On the outskirts of Makarov, the doors of a derelict garage swung open, and five vehicles drove out into the night. They headed in three directions. One truck drove up the coast to Vakhrushev and the naval docks, another drove inland and across the spine of the island to Il'inskiy, while the others, all armored, moved only a few blocks toward the computer center.

Despite massive efforts to find the SOBs, the roads they traveled were not busy with traffic. The ruddy-faced man in Russian uniform driving north up the coast saw few vehicles, but he traveled less than four miles before coming to the first roadblock. Two sentries who had been on duty for twelve hours without relief stood smoking at a barrier.

As the truck stopped and the driver rolled down the window, a young soldier walked to the driver's door. The other guard lounged against a tar-paper shack.

"Your papers, Comrade," the youth demanded.

O'Toole had one hand on his Beretta as the tired youth examined his papers casually.

"They giving you any rest?" O'Toole asked. "I've not seen my bed for more than a day."

"We've been here for twelve hours without relief," the youth replied, handing back the papers. "If they don't catch those bastards soon, we'll all be sleeping standing up."

"How's the hunt going, Comrade?" O'Toole asked. "They have me driving all the time. Never tell me anything."

"Who knows. I just hope they don't come this way." As the youth spoke, he walked to the barrier and raised it to let the truck pass.

O'Toole was glad he didn't have to start firing. He wanted to return through the checkpoint later and didn't want to find the Soviets investigating.

Five miles farther up the road, he spotted a sentry leaning against one building in a block of barracks. It was a military compound back from the road about fifty feet. He wheeled the truck up to the gate and waved the sentry over.

The guard moved slowly, opened the gate and walked toward the truck with his automatic rifle held in both hands. He slid back the cocking lever. The sound was ominous in the silence of the night.

O'Toole didn't wait to see if the Russian was serious. The Irishman's Beretta coughed twice, punching holes in the guard's forehead, tearing off the back of his head. O'Toole jumped from the truck and dragged the soldier behind a clump of trees.

He wasted no time. From his rucksack he took three of the C-4 molds he'd prepared, turned the timers for five minutes and placed them, one at a time, under the pilings of the first three barracks. He was back in the truck within seconds.

Liam O'Toole had a job to do, and he forced his tired mind to concentrate on the drive north. When the docks and the Russian warships loomed ahead, he was ready, his mind cleared by the monotony of driving. He'd have to find a way to get close to them. His job was to divert attention away from Makarov. He could set charges just for the effect, but that wasn't his style; he worked for maximum results.

As he drove up to the two sentries, he stroked the Beretta on the seat beside him. The silenced 93-R would be his constant companion and helper throughout the night.

THE MANEUVER HAD BEEN DISCUSSED thoroughly at the garage. The three armored vehicles changed course a block from the computer center, each coming at the building from a different direction. They had the advantage, but the didn't want the sound of a firefight to break the silence of the night.

Nanos rode with Barrabas, who steered his vehicle toward the front of the building from the east. Beck drove with Billy Two, who came at it from the west. As the vehicles roared up to the four sentries, Nanos and Beck, hidden until the last moment, cleared the armor and sprayed the four men with the last of their Socimi 9 mm slugs. The sentries went down like felled trees and lay still.

Hayes's task was more difficult. He was confronted by two guards at the rear of the building who had been alerted by the roar of powerful motors out front. Both men fired at the armored vehicle.

Hayes had the advantage of the protective armor, but they had the drop on him. He wasn't sure what his best move should be, so he continued to drive straight toward the two.

They ran.

As the machine caught up to one of the Russians, Hayes grasped the small Socimi with his free hand and sprayed 9 mm slugs wildly at the man as he fled. He went down, and Hayes drove over him, pressing the flesh into the soft earth.

At the front of the building, Nanos and Beck wasted no time. They scrambled out of the vehicles and raced across the road. Within a couple of minutes, the roar of powerful diesels could be heard over the idling of the armored cars.

Slowly the huge cranes came rumbling through the gates of the scrapyard and across the road toward the computer center. Reflected light from the fluorescents still on in the building provided a ghostly backdrop as the cranes with their round magnets dangling, crept closer. Finally they assumed positions on each side of the rectangular building.

While the cranes were started and wheeled into position, the armored cars formed a triangle covering the area with their 40 mm machine guns. The last thing the mercs had done in the garage was to mount the 40 mms above the armor for full traverse. Beside each man, a pile of Russian and Chinese AKs were loaded.

They had used some of Lee's surgical tape to produce Mag-Pac doubled magazines for speed-loading. Piles of the taped magazines lay at the warriors' feet alongside a full box of HE and phosphorous grenades. Each man had a rocket grenade launcher and a case of rockets. If they were attacked by armored vehicles, they would be on equal terms.

The crane operators started the generator diesels on their rigs and watched the voltage build. With the flick of a switch, the huge disks, one at the end of each crane, were activated, and the dynamic effect of the powerful electromagnets took effect.

In almost perfect harmony, the cranes swung the disks toward the lowest floors, moving forward to thrust the length of the structural steel neck of the cranes through the windows and slowly rake them from side to side.

As the work progressed, a series of explosions were heard to the north of the town. O'Toole was doing his job. Within minutes, they heard the scream of a dozen or more sirens heading north up the coast road. They continued to rake the cranes from one end to the other of the lowest floor.

Without warning, two trucks screeched to a stop at the front of the building. Barrabas and Billy Two raked the trucks with 40 mm steel-jacketed slugs. The two streams of steel tore at the men who were trying to escape the line of fire, and punched holes through the low-gauge steel until they found the gas tanks. The trucks blossomed into yellow and orange balls of flame, scorching everything on the ground, then rolling upward through the trees.

A dozen or more Soviets ran clear, dropped to the ground and rained a hail of 7.62 mm slugs off the steel plate of the SOBs' vehicles. Barrabas and Billy Two reached for HE grenades and lobbed a half dozen at the scattered survivors.

The silence that followed was broken by small arms fire from the rear. Barrabas and Billy Two could see Hayes's position. He was under fire from a platoon of infantry, pinned down while an armored vehicle lumbered into position for a frontal attack.

Barrabas had a clear line of fire. He rested the rocket launcher against armor plate, looked through the telescopic sight, checked the range for scale and rose a few inches above the armor to avoid the backlash.

He fired.

The missile screamed through the stand of young trees, missing by barely a foot. He reloaded, went through the procedure once more and sent a second rocket toward the enemy vehicle.

The rocket blew the vehicle and its occupants back ten feet, scattering hot metal throughout the undergrowth. In return, two enemy slugs hit Barrabas, one in each shoulder, throwing him backward and cracking his head against the opposite wall. He was stunned, but the Kevlar had saved him.

LESS THAN A MILE from the garage, Sanchez found himself driving toward another roadblock. There was only one way to go, and that was straight ahead.

As he neared the checkpoint, he slid back the partition separating the cab from the rear and called back to Lee Hatton.

"Checkpoint coming up. We'll have to blast our way through."

"How many?"

"Two. They're coming now, one to each side. Take the one on the passenger side."

José still had on a Soviet uniform. He found cigarettes in the pocket and was lighting one when the face of a guard appeared on the other side of his window. When the Russian's gun also was shown, he pointed his Beretta and blew the face away. To his right, he heard a cocking lever slide home and felt the hair at the back of his neck start to rise. Two quick coughing noises followed the metallic sound of the lever. The Russian disappeared from view, and Lee's slim hand holding the Beretta, snaked back into the rear of the truck.

Sanchez opened the windows to let the smell of cigarette and powder dissipate. The Puerto Rican airman drove south on the coastal road, slipped down to second gear and slowed until no traffic showed ahead. Then he turned inland, lights off, through rolling brushland close to the north perimeter of the airfield.

"We're at the north fence," Lee told Sanchez. "I'm going to do a recon. I may be gone a half hour or more."

"I'll come, too," Sanchez insisted.

"Uh-uh. You stay. We need you intact. You're the only one who knows how to fly a plane."

She slipped from the cab and pulled off the Russian uniform. Now, except for the shoes, she was the SOB who landed at Mys Aniva forty-eight hours before. She had her knife and Beretta, as well as a Socimi with one magazine and two HE grenades. If she couldn't take the airport with those, they would all be in trouble.

Unencumbered by the heavy greatcoat, she jogged the four miles to the front gate in twenty minutes. Time was her enemy. She still had more than an hour to get the mercs on a plane, but it was slipping away fast.

A hundred yards from the front gate, Lee crouched behind some brush and watched the four Soviet guards. Two had the usual AK automatic rifles, but the other two were in an old armored halftrack with a monster 60 mm cannon mounted on a platform on its rear.

As she watched, a series of explosions broke the silence, bringing the Soviets to instant attention, their hands going for their weapons.

O'Toole was at work. Lee knew she would have to look at the rest of the perimeter. She jogged to the back gate where two guards patrolled along the inside of the fence. She had no way to get in. While she was thinking about the possibilities, a dog, tied on a long lead next to the guardhouse, started to bark and pull in her direction.

The guards let the dog go, and it tore to the fence where Lee hid.

The Russians saw her and opened fire. Two slugs hit her Kevlar, pushing her into the brush. She unclipped a grenade, pulled the pin and let it fly in a high arc over the fence.

The small ball of metal flew high and exploded over the sentries' heads. They died looking up.

The dog whimpered and trotted over to them, licking their faces, unable to understand why they wouldn't get up.

Lee pulled herself from the brush, stunned from the two shots on her Kevlar vest. She was disoriented and didn't know how much time had passed. She shook her head to clear it, and found herself looking into the muzzle of the 60 mm not fifty yards away.

THE FIRST EXPLOSIONS BROKE the silence of the night south of Vakhrushev at 0220. Colonel Nekrasov was lying on a couch in his office in Yuzhno-Sakhalinsk, almost a hundred miles away. A frightened messenger awakened him and told him the news.

"What are you saying? Speak up, man," the colonel said rubbing his eyes.

"A series of explosions up the coast, Colonel. Some barracks." The man stuttered it out, almost petrified with fear. Like most of his friends, simple farming folk, he did not fit into military life.

"How far up the coast? *How far?*"

"They mentioned Vakhrushev, Colonel. The barracks."

"Call for a helicopter. Tell Sergeant Kerugan to drive my staff car up, and I'll fly," he said, his voice cracking as he reached for a bottle of vodka in a lower drawer of his desk and then poured three fingers into a glass. When the liquid had burned down his throat, he picked up the phone.

"Get me Major Obolensky right away," he commanded the operator.

"The major called, but we would not disturb you, Colonel," a voice said back to him. "We knew you needed your sleep, Colonel."

"Fool! What did he want?"

The operator told him that the major would be at the barracks south of Vakhrushev when he could get there.

Furious that the KGB would be at the scene before him, Nekrasov rushed out of the building to the park across the street where a helicopter was waiting, its blades turning slowly, its red dome light flashing.

As he entered the helicopter and belted up, Nekrasov looked at his watch. Zero two-forty hours. Didn't these foreign commandos ever let up? he asked himself.

By 0300, he was over the scene and could see the wreckage of three barracks down below. The site was a flaming pyre.

The bastards!

He raised a microphone off a hook and thumbed the Talk button. "This is Colonel Nekrasov. Connect me with Major Obolensky," he commanded.

A voice from the area of the fire responded from a mobile communications truck. "The major has gone to Kakhrushev, Colonel. There have been more explosions further north."

"North," he ordered his pilot. "Look for more fires."

They were above the naval yard within five minutes, and once again they were looking down on a burning inferno. Nekrasov couldn't contain his rage. He pulled the mike from its hook pushed the Talk button and screamed, "Connect me with Major Obolensky."

They knew his voice. Major Obolensky, who was standing near the communications truck, was on the line in seconds.

"Obolensky? This is Nekrasov. What the hell's going on?"

"Sabotage, Colonel. Three barracks. I don't know how many men yet. Three of our new high speed missile boats," Obolensky said. "I'm not sure what's going on. Could have been only one man or a dozen. The fires could be a diversion."

"I'm coming down. Wait right there," the commanding officer said.

"Wait a moment, Colonel. Something new is coming in."

Nekrasov waited, fidgeting with the mike in his hand. Finally, the loudspeaker close to his ear broke the relative silence.

"Three more explosions, Colonel. South of Makarov. Close to Bykov. What do you want me to do?" Obolensky asked.

"I'm going to Bykov. You come down in convoy. Watch for anything suspicious heading north."

The bastards! How the hell was he going to catch up with them? They were always one step ahead.

16

The ride down from Vakhrushev had been less trouble than O'Toole anticipated. By the time he headed out at 0300 hours, every vehicle with a siren was screaming north. No one seemed interested in a dirty olive-green army truck heading south.

His targets at Bykov were the generating plants that supplied power to the whole island.

O'Toole was beginning to look very harassed. He was haggard, hadn't shaved and had pouches under his bloodshot eyes. He looked at his watch. Almost 0300. He would continue the diversions for another thirty minutes then start for the airport.

The power plants were heavily patrolled and ringed with high chain-link fences. He toured the area, finding the guards' barracks and the commandant's house.

The Irishman parked the truck in a new growth of pine behind the commandant's house and walked the fifty yards to the back of the dwelling. He placed a small C-4 charge next to an oil tank and set a timer for five minutes. Then he hurried to the guards' barracks a hundred yards away and knelt beside its five-hundred-gallon fuel tank.

"What are you doing?" a voice demanded in Russian.

"Checking for leaks," he shouted back.

The man was wearing civilian clothes; he was not a member of the guard detail. He was also no fool. Without hesitation, he drew his Makarov automatic and fired at O'Toole before the redhead could draw his Beretta.

A slug hit his chest and knocked him backward. A second slug tore at his pants, peeling a thin strip of skin from his leg. A third shot splashed into the puddle beside him as he rolled and drew his piece.

One shot from the Beretta passed through the Russian, pushing him back into the barracks and out of sight. O'Toole didn't follow up. He had to get the hell out of there.

The leg wound was minor. He circled to the left around the barracks on the side farthest from the power plants. As he ran toward the plant along a stand of trees, the first charge blew. The guards stood looking at the ruined house in awe. The second charge blew, and with it the oil tank. An instantaneous ball of fire billowed out, sweeping through the frame building. Men screamed and jumped from windows, their clothes aflame.

The whole power plant detail took off in panic, running across the lawn that separated the plants from the barracks. O'Toole started along the stand of trees. When he came to the end of the row, he angled toward the nearest open gate.

It was not going to be a fancy job. He had four molds of C-4 prepared, with the timers already implanted. As he ran through the gate, he pulled the first mold from his pack and pushed it against a huge transformer. He ran around inside the fence, placing the charges randomly, not caring if he picked the most vital spots. Each charge was set for five minutes, so he kept up a steady pace until he reached the safety of his truck. It had taken him less than three minutes.

The truck started without a problem. O'Toole threw it into first gear and pulled away as the first charge blew. Seconds later the second charge exploded, and the plant was engulfed by a giant mushroom cloud.

A shock wave hit the remnants of the guards' barracks as O'Toole's truck passed behind it. Shards of flaming wood struck the truck like a barrage of shells.

He drove north again, intending to set his last charges closer to Makarov. The traffic flow had reversed. Scores of fire engines and official cars were tearing south to the new conflagration. The only vehicle that was pointed in his direction was a black limousine with pennants flying, and even it was stopped with a flat tire.

O'Toole pulled behind the long black limo. He thought it might be to his advantage to change vehicles. The driver, a sergeant, had the tire off and was struggling to get the spare out of the trunk. He was bent over in pain, obviously not fit for the job he had to do.

"Can I help?" O'Toole asked as he stepped from the truck.

Sergeant Kerugan looked over his shoulder and dropped the wheel back into the trunk, holding his back as he tried to straighten.

"You can, soldier. This is Colonel Nekrasov's car. I'm supposed to follow him up the coast where he's waiting for me." He wiped his brow, reached into his hip pocket for a flask and drank deeply.

O'Toole reached into the trunk for the wheel, pulled it out with one hand and started to put it in place.

"Tell me about our esteemed colonel. Is he easy to work for?" O'Toole asked.

"He's a weak fool," Kerugan said, holding the flask out to O'Toole.

"That's dangerous talk," O'Toole said, ignoring the flask to help the sergeant take the jack from under the limousine. They threw it and the tools into the trunk and slammed the lid. "What if the wrong person heard you?"

"I don't give a shit. I've had it."

"I'm pleased to hear that," O'Toole said, drawing his Beretta. "Because from now on, you're working for me."

THE CRANES SMASHED through glass and pushed aside steel casements as they progressed through the interior of the buildings from one end to the other. Nanos and Beck were becoming expert at avoiding supporting pillars and they swept the huge electromagnets along shelves of tapes destroying every scrap of recorded data with their powerful magnetic fields.

Barrabas could see the progress. Nanos and Beck had worked smoothly throughout, ignoring the heavy gunfire even though steel-jacketed bullets hit the cages of their cranes. The second floor lay in waste.

They had fought off two attacks. Barrabas knew the enemy had to have radioed for more help. He could see Hayes and Billy Two working steadily, preparing for the next attack, making sure their rocket grenades were primed, the 40 mm guns fresh-loaded, the pile of AKs at their feet and the boxes of grenades within easy reach.

They had been lucky so far. One shell inside the armored vehicles, or one grenade, and they were dead. Their supply of HE, phosphorus and rocket grenades would blow, and nothing would be left of them to identify. That was part of the job, the part that got the juices flowing—and they were flowing now.

The roar of diesel engines caught his ear. It had to be a strong force if he could hear the engines above the noise of the cranes. And then, through the smoke of battle, Barrabas saw them. Two T-55 tanks on Hayes's flank and two on his. Behind the tanks there was probably a full company with another in reserve, he thought. This was going to be the final battle.

Hayes opened fire first with his rocket grenade and took out the tank closest to him. The other three tanks opened fire. One shell ripped into the computer building and exploded in the middle of the ground floor.

Nothing happened for a few seconds. As Barrabas and Billy Two lined up their RPGs, the tanks started to withdraw. Barrabas was puzzled. They knew how valuable the computer center was and couldn't risk destroying it themselves. He had been puzzled by the lack of helicopter gunboats. Now he knew. They'd have to rely on foot soldiers to take the SOBs' armored vehicles.

It started out as a wave of brown uniforms. Hayes, Billy Two and Barrabas all went to their 40 mms and set up a withering cross fire that halted the brown wave. Wild firing from reluctant troops sang off steel as they barely missed the SOBs.

Fresh waves of men climbed over fallen comrades only to be met by the scything flay of 40 mm slugs. As they retreated from certain death, the SOBs followed up with HE grenades.

The third battle had been won.

Barrabas waved to Hayes and Billy Two in the other armored cars. They waved back. They were fit and ready for the next attack. The cranes continued their work on the third floor. One to go. Barrabas glanced at his Rolex. It was 0315. They'd have to move fast. He drove his armored car out of position, surveyed the scene and motioned for Nanos and Beck to speed up. They backed the cranes for an assault on the top floor.

LEE HATTON LOOKED down the barrel of the 60 mm gun.

She wondered in the last seconds of her life how much pain she would have to bear. She was curious.

The gun moved slightly to line up on her. She steeled herself for death, her head proud, her chin out.

The noise was deafening. The halftrack exploded in a ball of flame and twisted metal. No one inside had even had time to scream.

She looked toward the truck, which José had driven to the back gate. Sanchez straddled the top of the twelve-foot fence, the long tube of the RPG-7 awkward in his hand. He grinned.

As she started to glance away, she heard the bark of an AK from behind the burning vehicle. She could see puffs of dust from José's Kevlar vest, and life seemed to leave him as he dropped the rocket tube and hung lifeless on the fence. She unclipped her last grenade and let if fly over the fence to eliminate the last of the enemy. Silence came to the airport once more.

Hatton sat for just a moment. The lifeless eyes of the hapless guard dog stared at her, its bloody tongue hanging from one side of its mouth.

It was only a few seconds since Sanchez had been hit. She picked herself up, raced around the fence and climbed.

Sanchez hung like a limp doll. Carefully she ripped the fabric of his coat and strained against his weight to lower him gently.

She laid him out on the grass. He was still breathing. Two bullets had gone through his thighs without breaking bone. He was bleeding, but he was alive.

Lee carried him to the truck and turned on a dome light. She found her bag and applied compresses to each wound, packing them and using a sling on each as a pressure bandage. She covered the wounds with sulfa dressings and stopped the bleeding. He was still out.

Lee heaved a sigh. It was hopeless. How the hell could she get him aboard an airplane? And even then, how could he fly?

But she had to try.

She got behind the wheel of the truck and drove to the gate. A strong lock secured it. She rummaged around in the truck for a grenade. All but one had been used. She sprinted back to the spot where Sanchez had been shot, picked up the rocket tube and returned to the truck. She loaded the rocket grenade and blew a hole in the gate.

She drove through the gate. Find a plane. Get the people on board. Break open the front gate. The tasks spun wobbly around in her tired brain like a broken recording tape.

She toured the whole airport and found it deserted. An old control center was visible in the dark at one side of the enclosure—deserted, or so it seemed. In front of the old building, three planes stood in the dark of night, none impressing her with their beauty.

One looked like an old Dakota. Another was a prop plane that looked like it had seen better days.

She looked over the third. It would have to do. It was a passenger jet, bigger than they wanted, something like a DC-9. It was a Tupolov TU-124. She stopped beside it, pushed a set of steps to the front hatch with brute strength and climbed the stairs.

Inside it was dark. She fumbled her way to the left seat and slipped into the soft leather. She tried a few switches, and the dials responded. The batteries were working. They had about a quarter load of fuel. Okay. They didn't have far to go. So much depended on Sanchez. Could he fly? Would this thing start without an auxiliary booster? She didn't have the answers.

Lee looked at her watch. It was 0320 hours. She had only forty minutes. She raced down the steps and back to the truck. Sanchez's eyes were open. He seemed to be stronger, but as Lee lifted him, he groaned and passed out again. She eased the Puerto Rican into the left seat and snapped the seat belts on to keep him from collapsing on the controls.

It was all she could do for now.

FLAMES BEGAN TO WANE, and smoke rose in white clouds through streams of seawater poured on charred hulls. Colonel Nekrasov turned in his seat for a last look. The pilot turned the MI-21 a hundred and eighty degrees and headed south.

Below, a steady stream of lights bounced down the coastal highway, some with flashing dome lights, and all exceeding normal speed limits to get to the scene of the latest explosions. The colonel felt he was at the end of a whip, being cracked at the owner's will, always too far from the hand to see who was wielding the length of leather.

He had issued orders for all troops to be mobile, and had heard reports that some action was taking place at the computer center, but he was not worried about that. He had sent tanks and two companies of regulars to the center. They would have it under control by now.

The crew he had to trap was the one setting these bombs. The results were not devastating in themselves, but they were bound to demoralize his whole force. Things had been bad enough before these attacks. Popolov had made his life miserable; the men had been poorly disciplined.

It took fifteen minutes to reach the latest scene of devastation. The power plant at Bykov had been totally destroyed. The barracks were in flames. The commandant's house was a pile of ash glowing in the dark.

It was unusually dark. Except for the flames from the ruins below, no lights could be seen. All of the island from Vakhrushev south was without power. It would remain that way until auxiliary generators could be shipped in from the mainland.

This was the end for him. No excuses. He had squadrons of the most modern and destructive planes in the world. The most powerful ships in the navy were based at Sakhalin. But they had been defeated, and by what?

Nekrasov reached for the microphone. "Connect me with Major Obolensky," he ordered.

It took a couple of minutes for Obolensky to respond. When his voice came on, he sounded exhausted.

"Colonel? How does it look down the coast?" he asked.

"Don't bother to come, Major. Where are you now?"

"About ten miles north. I just passed your car. The sergeant was fixing a flat tire. Someone was already helping him, so we didn't stop."

"That's all I need. He'll probably go all the way to Vakhrushev, as ordered," Nekrasov said, then realized how little it mattered. "I suppose it doesn't matter," he said. "I may not be needing the car for some time."

Obolensky was beginning to feel the same kind of pressure the colonel was going through. He had thought Popolov's death would give him an opportunity, but this devastation would see the end of his career. "I suppose it really doesn't matter," he repeated.

"Any suggestions?" Nekrasov asked, his eyes on the flames pouring out of the power plant below. He didn't care that the radio relay operator was probably listening in. He didn't care much about anything.

"We have to keep going, Boris," Obolensky said. "Make sure airports are covered, our radar people on their toes, our squadrons on alert," Obolensky suggested.

They were defeated men, discredited men in their final throes of authority. They knew the horrors of the Gulag as well as any Soviet. They knew the rewards for failure.

17

With the Beretta in one hand, O'Toole patted the old soldier down for weapons and went over the car thoroughly. On the steering column, below the dash, he found an old German Luger. Under the driver's seat, a Makarov rested on the floor within easy reach.

"Where'd you get the Luger?" he asked. The Irishman didn't think that the sergeant looked old enough to have been in World War II.

"I was in Stalingrad, not quite old enough for the service," the veteran said. "but old enough to kill my first German and steal his gun."

O'Toole had mixed emotions about the man. He had been in the service all his life, and therefore could be the most deadly enemy the merc would ever encounter. Or he could be in it for the ride, having nowhere else to go. At any rate, he was going to be the tool that would see the Irishman through the rest of the night's work.

"Let's go," O'Toole said. He pulled the clip from the Luger, emptied it and slipped it home. "I'll keep the Makarov. Maybe it'll be my souvenir."

"Where to?" the sergeant asked.

He was being too cooperative. There was no way O'Toole was going to be fooled, but he would use him.

"Makarov."

The luxury car pulled onto the highway and headed north. They rode in silence for a few minutes. O'Toole watched the man constantly to be sure he wasn't doing anything to attract attention to them. Traffic was still rushing south, heading for the latest disaster. Road blocks had been set up at intervals. The staff car cruised through them without slowing down.

"You set all those charges?" the sergeant asked casually.

"That's my present assignment," O'Toole said, starting to relax for the first time that night. He'd been enjoying himself; he couldn't remember the last time he'd had an open order to destroy for diversion, to range as far afield as he had and pick his own targets.

"You could do me a favor." Again, the comment was casual.

O'Toole was wary. This wily old vet could be leading him up the path. "What?" he asked.

"Officer's training school at Makarov. Bastards keep turning them out like sausages."

"You don't like officers?"

"Been in the service since I was seventeen. I'm sixty. Never met one I liked. And I'll throw in a bonus. One block from the training school is a munitions dump. Been there since they started fortifying this place. All obsolete stuff."

This guy had to be the foxiest old vet O'Toole had met, or maybe he just didn't give a damn. O'Toole couldn't make up his mind. He'd been in the service for more than forty years. Some vets got that way, just didn't give a shit—lived from day to day taking orders and hating every minute. Some were wily enough to throw a wrench in the works occasionally just for their personal satisfaction. It was that way in most countries and had to be that way in the Soviet Union. He'd ride with it, but he'd always have a way out.

"Let's have a look at the training school," he said.

They were on the outskirts of Makarov when he made the statement. He looked at his watch. A half hour to takeoff. This would have to be fast—one for the school, one for the dump. He took two of the last three molds of C-4 from his rucksack and set the timers—one for five minutes and the other for eight.

"The timers are set. No changing our minds," he told the driver. He set the third to go in forty-five minutes and thrust it under the driver's seat. If he didn't catch up with the others by 0400, they'd both meet their new commanding officer in whatever hell they'd made for themselves.

Sergeant Kerugan drove the limo past the sentry and up to a dormitory with total disdain for authority, as he always did when driving the colonel. No one ever challenged him.

Whey they were out of sight of the sentry, O'Toole slipped from the car, planted the bomb and was back in the seat in seconds. His Beretta had been trained on the old vet all the time, but he couldn't have gotten off a good shot. The sergeant had not made a move.

"Let's go," O'Toole said as he picked up the second mold. "Make it fast. We've got about three minutes to plant the next one and take off."

As promised, the munitions dump was close by. Two sentries waved them through casually. No one had visited the place for weeks. They might have thought it strange that their colonel would be visiting in the middle of the night, but they weren't about to stop him and risk annoying him.

This was one hell of a place to get trapped, O'Toole thought to himself as the car drove its way through stacks of old naval shells and crates of obsolete explosives. He took no chance, exited the car by the left door and placed the C-4 on a pile of crates. He took his eyes off the old soldier for less than two seconds in the process.

The man didn't try anything. When the Irishman climbed back in, he drove the limo sedately out of the compound, just as the officer's dormitory blew up. O'Toole saw the expression on the faces of the two guards through the dark glass of his window as they passed. He looked back when they were fifty yards down the street. They had figured it out. Instead of firing on the limo, they were getting the hell out, running as fast as they could.

The computer center was just three blocks away to the northeast. From where he sat, O'Toole could see it ringed around with troops.

"Where to?" Kerugan asked calmly.

"Il'inskiy."

"The airport?"

"The airport."

THE CRANES WERE STILL RAKING the third floor, with just the fourth to go. In one of the infrequent lulls in the fighting, Barrabas had looked at his watch. It had 0330 hours and that must have been five minutes ago. They weren't going to make it. They'd have to pass on the top floor.

His main worry had been an encounter with heavy armor, and that had been solved for him by the Soviets. They were afraid to destroy the computer center with random shells from their own guns. But there were other weapons they could have used. He knew he was pressing his luck. They'd be bound to start using something heavier soon.

He thought about this and the problem of their retreat while pouring hundreds of rounds of 40 mm steel-jacketed slugs at the enemy. The three of them had formed a routine. From their triangle, they kept up a steady wave of fire like a giant pinwheel. Every few minutes they would let the 40 mms cool. They'd pick up AKs and spray the advancing troops, picking them off in groups. When they attacked in heavier concentrations, all three SOBs lobbed fragmentation grenades at them, piling them up like cordwood, making it more difficult for the next wave to advance.

As he feared, they were finally using more sophisticated weapons. Through the smoke of battle, Barrabas could see motorized antitank weapons being pulled into position.

A shell whizzed past his head, not missing by more than a foot. They had all been hit by small arms fire, but always in the area of protective Kevlar. The shrapnel Barrabas had taken at the fish warehouse began to bother him. The places where the Kevlar had taken a hit were bruised and sore. The whole team was going to need some well deserved R&R when this was over.

No time for random thoughts. Time to get the hell out of there. In the millisecond the thought took to pass through the tissue of his active brain, a massive explosion shook the earth around them, blocking out all other sound. At the same moment, an antitank shell hit Billy Two's armored vehicle. The gunner's aim had been spoiled by the outside explosion, but the effects of the shell lifted the vehicle off the ground and threw the Osage clear. He lay exposed to enemy fire.

Another explosion rocked the earth and then another. The night sky was illuminated like the effect of a hundred rockets at the county fair. The noise was a hundred times louder, and the earth shook enough to topple frail buildings.

The cranes bounced off the ground. Nanos and Beck started to climb down from the cabs. Barrabas drove his vehicle to pick up Beck while Hayes went for Nanos. Billy Two didn't move.

Everyone was distracted by the massive explosions just two blocks away. Men fell to the ground, holding their hands over their heads as shards of steel rained down around them.

Barrabas breathed silent thanks to O'Toole for his handiwork as he drove the armored car around the building to pick up Billy Two. Beck had a Mag-Pac clip in an AK-56-1 and was giving cover fire. Some of the enemy saw what was going on and picked up the weapons they'd dropped, only to be downed by Beck's withering fire and the 40 mm Nanos had claimed for his own.

Barrabas shouted to Beck to toss phosphorous grenades into the lower floor as they made one final circle of the building. Nanos followed suit, and as they turned to leave, the once proud building became a sheet of flame.

Billy looked like a goner, but Barrabas hopped from his vehicle and lifted the lifeless form into it. He wheeled around and waved for Hayes to follow, choosing a way out that would lead to the the mountains and the road to Il'inskiy.

With eyes red and streaming from the smoke and heat, he pointed the nose of the armored car in the direction of the massive explosions that were giving him cover and drove the powerful vehicle forward. He pushed the steel monster through the ranks of the living, bowling them over like sheaves in the wind, and fought his way toward the hell of fire and brimstone that was still shaking the earth and punishing the ear.

As they moved closer to the hell that had been a munitions dump, they could see only one vehicle approaching. A bright yellow fire truck that was manned by a half-dozen firemen was cruising slowly toward them, looking for a place to set up and go to work.

Barrabas waved to Hayes and pointed to the fire truck. Beck and Nanos sprayed it with a deadly hail of steel. The firemen jumped down and fled. The SOBs took over the fire truck, and with sirens screaming and lights flashing, they tore through the night toward the airport.

It was 0345.

LEE HATTON HAD DONE all she could for the moment. She looked at her watch. Zero three forty-five. Sanchez had been drifting in and out of consciousness for more than twenty minutes. She might as well have been alone. The pilot was in place in his familiar left seat, but his eyes were closed, and his skin felt cold and clammy.

Zero three forty-eight. They would be arriving in a few minutes if they were arriving at all. She tried to revive Sanchez by slapping his cheeks lightly and rubbing his wrists. He opened his eyes and looked at her, dazed.

"What's going on?" he asked, his voice weak.

"You took one in each thigh. They were 223s. The entry holes aren't big, but you lost a lot of blood before I could get it stopped." She knelt in front of him and looked into his face.

The Puerto Rican grimaced as the pain stabbed through his body.

"I'll give you some morphine," Lee told him in comforting tones. She took a vial from the bag, rummaged for a syringe and sucked the clear liquid deftly into the plastic tube. Holding the needle up to the light, Lee carefully pressed the plunger to squeeze out any remaining air. A drop of morphine ran down the needle. Quickly she pinched an inch of flesh, and rammed the needle home.

"How's that?" she asked, as relief slowly flooded the pilot's face.

"Feels better already," José said. "Think I can fly this bird out of here?"

"I'm hoping."

"Baby, ain't nothing going to stop me now."

Lee couldn't resist a smile. The powerful dose of morphine had brought back José's sense of humor.

"Start 'em up," Lee told him. "Taxi to the main gate."

Sanchez already had his hands on the control bar. He flicked on the ignition for the port motor and turned the starter button beside it. The motor coughed, stalled, then revved to life. It sounded rough at first, but finally settled down to a steady rhythm.

The wounded man reached for the starboard motor switches and went through the same routine. He tried three times, and the only response from the motor was a cough. It wasn't going to start. Neither was the pilot. Sanchez had passed out again, his chin on his chest.

Lee Hatton looked at her watch. Zero three fifty-five. They had to get the damned thing started.

She raced to the outer door, down the steps and to the truck she'd left on the tarmac. She drove the few hundred yards to the administration building and the small maintenance buildings nearby. In front of one, a booster truck was parked, its cable coiled over the driver's seat. She started the diesel generator motor, then the truck's motor. Both came to life with a roar and a stream of blue smoke.

At the plane, she plugged in the booster truck, moved back to the cockpit and slapped Sanchez to life.

"Come on! I can't do it all!" she screamed at the pilot.

"What?" the befuddled Sanchez asked.

"The starboard engine. Try it now," Lee said, trying to keep her head. She looked at her watch. Zero three fifty-nine.

Sanchez flipped on the switch and turned the starting lever. The motor coughed twice, protesting against use without maintenance, then settled into a steady throb.

Hatton went outside and disconnected the booster truck in seconds. Back in the cockpit, she yelled over the sound of the motors, "Taxi to the main gate. You'll see it straight ahead."

Slowly, as Sanchez released the brakes and revved up, the old jet began to rumble along the uneven asphalt toward the gate. They had about a half mile to go and were making it at about ten miles an hour. They were too slow. It was 0400.

Sanchez revved the motors higher. They bounded along the tarmac at about twenty miles an hour...three hundred yards to go...two hundred...one hundred. His chin slumped onto his chest, and he pulled the control column to one side. The plane veered away from the gate in a full circle barely in time before the tired old motors stalled.

COLONEL NEKRASOV SAT in his office, looking out on the darkened square, his eyes dull from lack of sleep. He could hear the explosions reverberating across the island. He'd had a report of the officer's training school and the ammunition dump. The invaders had destroyed the computer center and had broken through the troops he'd massed around the center to entrap them.

What kind of animals were they? They should have died at Mys Aniva under the first hail of fire, but they had not. They should have died at the warehouse, but they had escaped down a hatch and under the docks by boat. He'd seen the warehouse. No one should have survived the devastation there. No one should have escaped the massacre at the computer center, but they had.

Worse, they had made a fool of him. He'd been entrusted with one of the most important installations in the Soviet Union, and he'd let what had to be a handful of men destroy it. A handful of men! A dozen— maybe less.

He knew the consequences of failure. Any failure at his level was an end to progress. It wasn't fair. He'd had no chance from the beginning. Most of his resources were designed for massive attack from the sea. He didn't have unlimited foot soldiers for internal defence. It wasn't fair.

He moved from his desk to the small washroom off his office, turned on the battery-operated emergency light and looked at the haggard face in the mirror. He took off his jacket, tie and shirt, ran hot water into the bowl and reached into the cupboard for his razor.

When he had shaved, he combed his hair carefully, put on his shirt and tie and returned to his desk. The sky was as dark outside as it had been before. The whole south end of the island was without power.

The doomed Colonel knew he could not escape the Gulags, those horror camps filled with dissidents and unfortunate men like himself. He picked up the telephone. In the darkened office, he could barely see the dial. He dialed zero and asked the operator to connect him with General Persof of Moscow.

After six rings, a sleep-drugged voice answered.

"Persof."

"General?"

"Who the hell is this?"

"Colonel Nekrasov at Sakhalin."

"What the hell do you want at this time of night, Colonel?" Persof asked. "Are you under attack? Have the Americans retaliated?" The general looked at his watch, sat up in his bed and lit a cigarette.

"You might say that, General," Nekrasov said, drawing his holstered automatic.

"Goddammit, man! Explain! What the hell's going on?

His answer was a muffled explosion at the other end of the line.

The old soldier sat still for a minute, smoking. Something very big was going on at Sakhalin.

He reached the operator again and gave him the number his son had left.

18

Barrabas drove the fire truck, which was both a ladder truck and a tanker. Nanos clung to the side rails next to Barrabas to act as interpreter. Hayes clung to the other side with Billy Two at his feet. No one had been able to check the Osage over. He didn't look good. Blood dripped from his nose and ears. As far as they could tell, he was still alive. When they arrived at the airport, Lee would have a look at him.

Beck had taken the time when they switched vehicles to throw a half-dozen 56-1s on the fire truck with a dozen Mag-Pacs and a box of grenades. The fighting should be over, but they couldn't be sure. He had found a flat area at the back of the truck to sit and arm the weapons.

The area around the computer building was blocked off by army units trying to get into the fight. No one could move effectively while the munitions dump continued to blow. Barrabas used the siren while Nanos screamed at officers who wanted them to turn back toward the munitions dump. While they crawled along, not two blocks from the flaming dump, a mammoth explosion rocked the area, and a shower of fire rained from the sky for three blocks in every direction.

The men who had been shouting at them suddenly turned into torches and ran screaming, bumping into each other, their clothes and hair aflame.

The SOBs couldn't breathe.

"This thing's got to have masks," Barrabas shouted. He stopped the truck, dropped to the ground and started opening all the compartments that lined the sides of the vehicle.

Heat built up, scorching their lungs. They coughed as they tore open one compartment after another. Beck moved Billy to the back and threw a fireman's cape over him.

"I've got them!" Hayes called from his side of the truck.

They scrambled to grab a mask and tank. Beck, who was looking after the fallen Osage, grabbed two sets. They were the only ones breathing clean air within a thousand yards.

When Hayes took his first breaths from the tank, his head cleared. He realized they were going to fry, along with everyone else. He pulled a hose from a reel on his side, opened a valve and started to spray the water over their heads. On the other side, Nanos followed his lead as Barrabas resumed his seat behind the wheel.

Under a fine spray, the truck moved ahead through the fire, the heat blistering everything not covered. The few Soviets who were not already dead from smoke inhalation or scorched lungs, ran in circles, their clothes smoldering and breaking into flames. Human torches were everywhere. They dropped and lay across the road, leaving Barrabas no alternative but to run them over as the smoke-stained yellow truck moved slowly westward toward the mountains and clear air.

SERGEANT KERUGAN REMAINED a mystery to O'Toole. He drove calmly out of Makarov, as if he were on one of his regular assignments with his colonel.

"I have heard Americans always talk of freedom. What does that mean to you, soldier?" he asked.

"How can I explain freedom to you?" O'Toole asked, speaking as much to himself as to his driver. "We are not responsible to the state. The state is responsible to us. If we don't like what the leaders are doing, we change the leaders."

The sergeant was silent for a few minutes. "We change leaders, too." He thought for a few seconds. "No," he said. "The leaders change each other. We change nothing. Do you think we will ever understand one another, Comrade?" he asked.

The "comrade" was not lost on O'Toole. The Irishman, the most down-to-earth of all the SOBs when not on a job, was warming to the Russian, but one part of his brain was still telling him to go easy.

He looked at his watch. It was 0400. He was late. Barrabas had warned everyone that they would not wait. He looked down at his feet. The C-4 he'd set to blow at four-fifteen was still in place.

LEE HATTON DROPPED to the asphalt and started to run. In long loping strides, she headed back to the terminal building and the booster truck. For the first time, she felt truly alone and helpless. She had her commando knife and the Beretta and the skills she'd learned from her father, the famous U.K. Army general. But she felt helpless.

She knew she could survive alone. It would be easy to get to the sea and find a boat. Or she could live off the land and keep out of sight.

But she was not alone.

Hatton looked at her watch. It was past four. Where the hell were they?

She ran like a creature of the forest. Her breathing was normal, her heartbeat regular, her muscles loose and fluid. The booster truck loomed in the night. She slowed, climbed behind the wheel and pressed the starter.

For the second time she turned the machine toward the aircraft.

THEY PASSED OUT OF THE WORST of the fire zone and shut down the hoses. Nanos leaned over to Barrabas and shouted through his mask, "What the hell blew?"

"Had to be a munitions dump. That last blast was phosphorous," Barrabas said. He concentrated on his driving for a few seconds. "It had to be O'Toole at work."

"We're late, Colonel!" Hayes shouted. "It's almost four. How long to the airport?"

"Who knows? If we don't run into trouble, we should be there in ten or fifteen minutes."

Beck passed one of the four AKs he had slung over one shoulder to each of the SOBs and then moved closer to the rear of the vehicle and the wounded warrior. Billy Two had stopped bleeding.

They slowly pulled out of the fire area and the ring of troops that had stayed clear. Officers waved them to stop and turn back, but Barrabas kept the machine pointed straight ahead.

They were finally free of the conflagration and the troops. The air was clear. They tossed off the masks and picked up speed.

LEE HATTON HOOKED UP the starter cable, kicked the diesel generator to life and hauled up the forward hatch into the silent aircraft. Sanchez was still immobile in the pilot's seat.

"Wake the hell up!" she screamed. She was losing control. The whole thing was hopeless. It was after four, and she didn't have the damned plane ready. How the hell could Sanchez get them out of there?

"José!" She slapped his face, gently at first, but with more force as his eyes stayed closed. "José! It's Lee! Wake the hell up!"

She reached into the bag and found a handful of small cloth-covered ampules of smelling salts.

She broke the glass, thrusting the sharp smelling salts under the pilot's nose in frustration. A hand knocked it away as Sanchez jerked awake. "What the hell you doing?" he snorted.

"You've got to stay awake, José," Lee said harshly. She was seated close to him and didn't have to strain against her straps to lean close to his ear. "You've got to get this plane ready for the others. It's the only way to get out of here."

"Sure." Sanchez shook his head to clear the cobwebs but only managed to bring on another round of dizziness. He reached for a starter button, and the port engine coughed into life, easier this time. He checked the gauges. The revs had increased, and the oil pressure was in the green.

He sat there, content with himself until Hatton spoke to him again. "We've got to get it moving, José. Let's see if it will taxi to the main gate," she urged.

The wounded man reached for the other starter button and the starboard engine roared, already warmed from the first try. He checked the revs and oil pressure, changed the mixture from lean to rich, and the two old motors settled down to a smooth pattern.

Hatton told Sanchez to hold off taxiing for a minute while she disconnected the truck. She was back in seconds.

"Okay, José. Move it!" she shouted from the bulkhead door. "The airport entrance is straight ahead. I'm going to try to get the stairs at the back door down."

The old Tupolov started to move, her lights out, surrounded by the darkness of a Sakhalin night.

19

Major Obolensky looked down at the dead colonel. He knew exactly what had gone through the man's mind. In his earlier years, he had been assigned to Western cities as an embassy attaché or a minor official. His work had always been KGB, always directed toward two things: constant observation of his own people's loyalty and recruiting new agents.

He had often met with and talked to people who lived under a democratic government. They had seemed casual, criticized their own system as well as his and were not worried about speaking freely against anything. He hadn't understood their attitudes then.

He understood them now. For the first time, he felt the long arm of communism reaching out for him, throwing out the net that would take him back to Moscow and finally the Gulags. Nekrasov had understood it and had chosen to end his life rather than face the disgrace and the horror of enslavement for the rest of his life.

He was not going to take the same route. He left the office, found the colonel's pilot in the outer office drinking vodka to calm his shaking hands.

"Are you fit to fly, Captain?" he asked. He meant no censure and needed a drink himself but hadn't the time. He had decided to fight the bastards who had done this to him.

"I'm okay, Major. The colonel's death was quite a jolt. Never thought he'd do it."

"Forget it. Is your bird ready to fly?"

"Sitting on the pad outside."

"Warm it up. I'm going to make a call."

When the captain had gone, Obolensky picked up the phone. "Give me Central Command," he told the male operator.

Within seconds another operator said, "Central Command."

"This is Major Obolensky. Who's in command?" he asked.

"Captain Metslov, sir. But he's at the computer center at Makarov."

"What's the report on Makarov?"

"It's not good, Major," the clerk on duty said. "The colonel had concentrated most of our land forces at the computer center. The report I have indicates heavy casualties. I can't reach an officer direct."

"What do your people tell you?"

"They're all dead, Major."

Obolensky had no idea that things were that bad. His order was slow in coming. "Those bastards don't plan suicide missions. I want new roadblocks every two miles down each coastal road. Double the guard at the airports."

"We don't have the people, Major."

"Tell the navy they have to release every ablebodied man. *We want these people, Sergeant,*" Obolensky screamed into the phone before he hung up.

He was shaking as he left the office. The atmosphere of the building was eerie. Dull emergency light from battery packs was minimal, barely allowing him to see. He walked down the steps to a small parade ground and a helipad. Outside, the only light came from the machine that was waiting for him, its rotors turning.

HEAVY WINDS BLEW IN from the Tatar Strait, coming off the mainland, whipping the strait into a white froth and curling up from the shore to the road along the coast. Gusts reached forty and fifty miles an hour as the wind swirled around rock outcroppings and bent trees over.

It was dark. Black storm clouds cut across the strait, driven by the winds, to add to the gloom. The only light the SOBs could see came from the white beams that cut through the night from their own vehicle.

They were ten miles from Il'inskiy and tearing down the coastal road at sixty miles an hour. Ten minutes, and they would be there. One mile ahead, three army trucks were pulled up, with two of them blocking the road.

Barrabas slowed. "We're going through!" he yelled over the rush of air that tore at their coats. "Hang on!"

Nanos and Beck cocked their AK-56-1s, wrapped one arm around a stanchion on the truck and aimed at the enemy. Beck hung on at the back, making sure

Billy Two didn't fall of as they bumped down the uneven highway.

When they came within range, slugs tore at the fenders of the rampaging yellow machine and shattered glass. Nanos and Hayes answered the fire with a steady stream of steel, as they yanked off Mag-Pacs, reversed them in seconds and continued the flow, shredding steel and glass, tearing into flesh and bone.

They were close. The shooters stopped firing and braced for the collision. They had used only a fraction of the water in the truck's tanks. The frame of the machine was braced to hold the weight when loaded. The front bumper, a curved sheet of half-inch steel, easily picked up the two smaller vehicles and, although slowed and dented, rolled on.

The third army vehicle, a staff car, swerved around the wrecks and began to gain on the lumbering yellow fire truck. Someone was trying to fire an AK from a front window, gave it up and held a Makarov out instead. Random shots struck the steel beside Beck.

The computer whiz, nursing the injured Osage, unslung his AK-1 and emptied a magazine at the car as it weaved to avoid his fire. He took out the windshield, but the car continued onward.

They were approaching another roadblock. Barrabas had increased speed but had to slow for the next encounter. Beck reached for the box of grenades that bounced on the steel platform beside him. He pulled a pin, waited, then threw it on the road behind. It bounced twice, then took a crazy hop over the pursuing car.

They were close to the next roadblock. Nanos and Hayes had fresh Mag-Pacs in their rifles. Beck pulled another pin and tried a bowling shot with reverse spin. The grenade bounced once, slowed by the spin, and flew straight through the shattered windshield.

As the running firefight started again, Nanos and Hayes emptied magazines at the enemy who sprayed the yellow engine with steel. Barrabas was the most vulnerable. Blood poured down his face from fragments of flying glass, almost distorting his view, but he was not hit. He had taken two more slugs in the Kevlar, but none had penetrated.

Three vehicles forming the roadblock drew up in close formation. Again the yellow engine tore through. The front bumper and fenders took a beating as they crushed the smaller vehicles. Rubber smoked as tires rubbed against jagged steel. The pursuing car, which had become a torch out of control, smashed into one of the overturned army trucks and exploded.

Through the wall of fire, two small army trucks screamed rubber on asphalt as they took off after the fire truck, now trailing smoke. They had only one mile to go.

THE HELICOPTER HAD CRUISED the east coast from Yuzhno-Sakhalinsk to Poronaysk. The power plant and surrounding buildings still smoldered. The fire pumps lacked power and the personnel to man them. The officer's training school and the barracks south of Vakhrushev still sent lazy columns of black and white smoke into the sky. The ships at the naval yard had sunk and could not be seen. Nor could the enemy.

They turned back toward Makarov and flew over the computer center. It was a mass of flame. Nearby, small explosions still lit the night sky, revealing several huge craters where the ammunition dump had once been.

Obolensky sat in the bubble, looking out over ninety degrees of destruction. He could not believe a handful of men could do so much damage without receiving some injury themselves. He couldn't be sure they hadn't died at the computer center. He'd had one report that they'd stolen a fire truck and had broken through hundreds of troopers. He was ready to believe almost anything.

Pointing to the north, he shouted to the pilot, "Fly north over the ridge to Boshnyakov and south down the coast."

THE TUPOLOV SAT ALONE, four hundred yards from the entrance to the airport, its engines warmed and idling, its nose pointed into the wind. Sanchez sat at the controls.

Lee Hatton was in the aft cabin trying to get the steps to work. She had the door open to the night wind, but she could not get the mechanism to lower the stairs to work. She couldn't do any more. Both fore and aft doors were open. The SOBs would just have to hoist themselves aboard as she had.

AS BARRABAS STRAINED to see through the blood that had dried on his face and clogged his eyes, a black limousine appeared out of the night in front of him, its pennants flying. It turned into the entrance to the airport.

An aircraft sat close to the massive steel gates of Il'inskiy Airport. Someone stood at the aft door, waving to them frantically. The limousine stopped. Liam O'Toole hopped out and swung aboard the yellow fire engine as it passed.

ABOVE THE ROAD, Obolensky peered through the endless black sky. The machine was buffeted by winds coming in from the stretch of water between Sakhalin and the mainland.

"We should put down, Major," the captain advised. "This crate was not built to stand winds like this." He had lost two close friends in this invasion already when they'd been ordered up in foul weather. He didn't want to meet the same fate.

Obolensky wasn't about to quit. He ignored the plea and pointed straight ahead down the highway where their twin headlight beams cut through the blackness. "What's that up ahead?" he asked.

They flew over the first roadblock. Two vehicles were crushed at the side of the road. Bodies lay near the wrecks. As he watched the first truck burst into flame, followed by the second. The scene was more vivid now, the wreckage another sample of the havoc the enemy had wrought.

"They're close!" he screamed at the pilot. He had to get these people. He had to get to them himself and stop them.

"We can't keep aloft in this air, Major. We've got to get out of it, set down!" the captain screamed through the roar of his rotors and the mad thrust of the wind.

Again Obolensky ignored him. He pointed straight ahead. The second roadblock was in sight. More burning vehicles. More dead bodies. It had been the same story for the past two days.

"Il'inskiy!" he screamed at the pilot. "Straight ahead. Il'inskiy! Stop them!"

HATTON SAW THE MERCS enter the gate. She raced to the front of the Tupolov and shouted desperately at Sanchez.

"Start the takeoff!" she shouted into his ear. "Get it up to about fifty and don't turn on full power until I signal."

Sanchez acknowledged with a nod. He pushed the power column forward and the plane began to roll, slowly at first then picking up speed to twenty, thirty, forty, fifty.

Barrabas steered the fire engine carefully behind the starboard wing keeping abreast of the two doors.

O'Toole and Beck lifted Billy Two and passed him through the rear hatch. Beck jumped and missed, catching the bottom of the door. Someone grabbed him and hoisted him in. O'Toole jumped and was caught by the same arms.

The two army trucks had pulled in behind and were firing wildly at the fire truck and the tail section, shredding some skin from the rear wing. Hayes used up his last Mag-Pac on the trailing vehicles, then climbed behind Barrabas to the left side of the truck and helped Nanos reach for the forward door.

Nanos made it into the door with O'Toole's help. Hayes picked up Nanos's AK and emptied it at the trucks behind, making them sway out of line to avoid his fire. Then he jumped to the front door to be caught and pulled in by O'Toole and Nanos.

Barrabas was last. He could barely see, but he had to perform a maneuver that would make a Hollywood stuntman cringe. He rubbed his eyes with the back of his hand, keeping the fire truck parallel with the plane. He eased himself to the left, held on to the steering wheel until the last second, then thrust the wheel to the right and jumped.

O'Toole caught him and pulled him aboard as the fire truck careered to the right and cleared the plane.

"Get the doors closed," the Irishman commanded as he ran forward "All right!" he screamed at Lee. "Tell Sanchez to get us the hell out of here!"

Outside, the two trucks were still in pursuit and were not losing ground. Their small arms fire was shredding the tail section. In a matter of seconds, the rear controls would be useless.

In the elegant black limo, Sergeant Kerugan was enjoying himself more than he had for years. He had liked the American. The man was not the monster that Americans had been portrayed as. True, he had killed many Russians, but he was a soldier under orders. This was something a military man could understand. Kerugan kept pace with the army trucks, not ten feet from them and directly behind the tail section. A heavy backwash from the two jet engines was beginning to make him weave from side to side. The black limo was difficult to control.

He stole a glance at the clock on the dash. The American had taken him at gunpoint at about 0330 hours. The second hand was just coming up to 0415.

In the air, the helicopter was fighting its way through ugly winds, trying to maintain stability. At fifty feet, winds gushed from the tarmac and attacked the rotors, making them roll erratically. The backwash from the jet engines didn't help.

"Get up ahead. If the trucks can't stop them, we'll land in front of them," Obolensky ordered.

"Major, I can't hold this thing," the captain protested. He was scared shitless.

Again Obolensky ignored the plea, intent on the kill. As he was about to repeat the order, the limo blossomed into a ball of orange and red flame, enveloping the two trucks in its conflagration. The shock wave turned the trucks away from the chase, their occupants charred by the flames.

The helicopter pilot could see he wasn't about to dissuade the major. He pulled ahead of the racing jet, and at the end of the runway made a one hundred-eighty degree turn. As he made the maneuver, at less than a hundred feet, a wind shear caught the rotors, robbing them of air. The machine dropped like a rock from the sky and exploded at the end of the runway.

With ten feet to spare, the Tupolov climbed over the wreck, reaching for calmer air.

20

The office on the top floor of the granite structure overlooking Dzerzhinsky Square was almost dark. The street below was cold, as winter started to send signals that it was on its way. Dried leaves, fallen weeks earlier from the trees of Moscow's parks, swirled in the eddies that formed between the buildings lining the square. The first snowflakes of the year had fallen, and the Russians walked hunched against the cold wind, knowing the ground would soon be covered.

The man behind the desk watched the smoke from his Havana curl toward the ceiling. A blanket was draped across an overstuffed divan against one wall. A tray of food sat half-eaten on a table in one corner. The huge man had not left the room in more than forty-eight hours, had not shaved, had not allowed his aides a moment to themselves since the SOBs escaped the ambush at Mys Aniva.

The President of the United States had been on the line with him five times since the Korean plane was shot down. He had listened to the insults and ranted back in turn, demanding restitution for the damage to the installations on Sakhalin. The Americans had claimed innocence, and the President had sounded convincing. Popolov's death had left his world in one hell of a mess.

Ladislov Buruka had called Sakhalin headquarters five times since midnight. Nekrasov had been touring the island, and now he'd learned from spies in Persof's office that the colonel was dead. The rest of General Persof's senior officers had been killed in a battle at the computer center. Obolensky had tried to keep him informed, but now the damned fool was off in a helicopter and had left no lines of communication open.

Buruka had ordered one of his protégés to the scene hours earlier. The journey, even by plane would take him hours. The fool had taken off on the run, never considering a military jet that would have flown him there in four. He was surrounded by fools. His predecessor had been a doddering fool. The premier was an old fool. Anyone who would transfer all state computer storage to a remote island was a fool. Even the American President knew the premier was powerless and had called Buruka repeatedly instead of his counterpart in the Kremlin.

He looked at his watch again. The last report claimed the invaders had been trapped on a coastal road and were about to be captured. He reached for the phone again.

WHEN THE PLANE CLEARED the burning helicopter, Barrabas struggled from the seat he'd taken at take-off and leaned against gravity as he climbed the sloping aisle to the cockpit. He found Lee Hatton in the engineer's chair, her face ashen. He knelt beside her.

"What the hell happened to Sanchez?" he asked, his face close to hers.

"Caught a couple in the legs, Colonel," she said, looking over at the blood-covered face. "Same question, Nile. Your face looks like it's been through a meat grinder."

"Just glass. No sweat," he said. "How's he doing?"

"See for yourself. I have to keep shouting at him to keep him awake."

Barrabas eased himself into the seat next to the Puerto Rican pilot and examined him with care. The man was flying by instinct. He was fighting blackout every second and looked as though he might not make it. As his eyes closed and his chin slumped on his chest again, Lee called to him, shook him by the shoulder. He opened his eyes for a few more seconds.

Barrabas had used flight simulators many years ago during military training. He'd had unusual reflexes and took to the stick like a natural. But he'd never gone beyond the simulated stage. He could fly the electronic plane like an expert, but he'd never done the real thing. None of the other SOBs had trained as pilots.

Suddenly, as they leveled off at about ten thousand feet, Sanchez slumped in his seat. The plane began to lose altitude. The Tupolov was over the Sea of Okhotsk, heading toward the Pacific. They were heading one hundred and eighty degrees off course with an unconscious pilot at the controls.

THE ROOMS AT OKHA and Dolinsk were filled with pilots drinking coffee and awaiting orders. At Okha, the proud new Foxhounds waited on the tarmac, serviced and ready to go. At the opposite end of the island, not far from the salvage operation in the strait off Mys Aniva, older aircraft, U-15s identical to the one that shot down the KAL commercial flight, were gassed, armed and ready.

No one had given an order to scramble. Flight control officers had been in conference with the island commandant earlier and had been ordered to join land forces to repel the invaders. A rumor persisted that the island commandant had taken his life. There were also reports that Popolov was dead.

They had all heard the explosions around the island. The pilots at Dolinsk, affected by the power blackout, sat in a gloomy atmosphere, the room lit by auxiliary lamps, their coffee brewed on an old propane stove. The flyers knew about the two downed helicopters, had known the men who died, but had not received their orders.

Something was very wrong, but until they had orders, they could do nothing.

THE BIRD DROPPED five thousand feet in what seemed like seconds. Barrabas grabbed the controls and tried to level her out. At three thousand feet, he had pulled back on the controls and had evened out the flight path but had not been able to change the course.

The only hope for them was to make a wide turn and head back over the fleet of ships still searching for the black box. From there it was only a small hop to the safety of an airstrip on Hokkaido.

"How's it going, Colonel?" Lee asked.

"Not good. Get Sanchez the hell awake, or we'll be swimming."

"He's in bad shape, Colonel." Hatton grabbed another vial of smelling salts.

"I can't fly this bird. You've got to wake him."

While he was talking, he eased the control bar over and tried a long sweeping turn to the right. The airplane was responding, but a glance at the altimeter confirmed she was slipping air. He gave her more power, correcting the loss, but the plane had taken them down to a thousand feet with a correction of only ninety degrees. Instead of north, they were now heading east, straight out to the Pacific.

BURUKA HAD BEEN MISINFORMED about many things, and one was the mode of transportation his aide had taken. A Foxhound A, their latest, was cruising at thirty-eight thousand feet over Sverdlovsk, expecting the first of two refueling tankers to show on radar any minute. The second would pick them up over Bratsk in an hour and a half.

Colonel Boris Kerensky was strapped into the rear seat of the Foxhound, going over in his mind the situation he would face when he got to Sakhalin. Popolov had died mysteriously. Nekrasov had killed himself. The south half of the island, at least, was in darkness. Most of the island's ground forces were dead or injured. Reports from Sakhalin claimed that the invading force had been less than a dozen men. They had to be wrong.

He signaled to the pilot. "Connect me with Sakhalin control."

In a few seconds, the voice of an operator filled his earphones.

"Sergeant Petunin, Colonel."

"Connect me with the highest ranking officer on the island."

"I cannot do that, Colonel. Major Obolensky ordered all officers to join the ground forces to fight the invaders."

"Is the man mad? Can you connect me with him?"

"He's dead, Colonel. He died a few minutes ago at Il'inskiy trying to stop the invader's plane from taking off."

Kerensky ignored the news of the major's death. He had to worry about the living. "So our squadrons are up? They should make short work of one unarmed jet."

"I can't affirm that, Colonel. Who would give the order?"

"Patch me into flight control," he shouted into his mike. Had everything gone mad on the island?

He had to wait for a full five minutes. The refueling tanker showed up on radar, five miles ahead. The Foxhound had slowed and was creeping up to the tanker's umbilical.

"Okha. This is Okha Flight Control. Identify." An exhausted sergeant sat at the communications console at Okha, waiting for something to happen.

"This is Colonel Kerensky of the Komitet Gosudarstvennoi Bezopasnosti. Connect me with your commanding officer at once," Kerensky shouted into his mike.

Two things about the call bothered the sergeant. First, he was at the mercy of a colonel who was calling from god knows where. Second, the man was KGB. It was the first time he hadn't been surrounded by officers in his adult life, and now this.

"We have no officers, Colonel, except for the flyers. With all respect, our officers were called out on special duty."

"This is *preposterous*." Kerensky was about to lose control. "All right. I want you to relay my personal orders. I want you to alert all radar installations to watch for a commercial jet that took off in the past hour. I want you to scramble a flight from Okha and one from Dolinsk."

"I'll have to confirm with Moscow, sir."

"Let me give you a word of advice, Sergeant. What is your name?"

"Mikhail Lomonosov, sir."

"Lomonosov, if you do not have two squadrons in the air in three minutes, I'll have your ass on a platter when I get there."

SANCHEZ WAS AWARE of the sharp sting of ammonia in his nasal membranes. He brought his hands up to push the source away and opened his eyes. Lee Hatton was bending over him, waving an ampule of smelling salts under his nose.

Airplane, he thought, dimly aware of the morphine-numbed pain in his legs. Got to fly this airplane. He clicked on like a light bulb, grabbing the controls and sighting the plane until it began to ascend.

"Glad to have you back!" Barrabas grinned with obvious relief in the seat beside him.

Sanchez nodded, concentrating on flying the plane.

Lee left them and went to the back of the plane to examine Billy Two.

THE FOXHOUNDS STARTED to move along the tarmac toward their runway, evil looking creatures born out of the hell that was war. Predawn mists shrouded them in white cotton that swirled before them, then disappeared in the blast of their jets. One after the other, they climbed toward open sky above the black overcast that still enveloped the island.

A radar fix had been recorded a few minutes earlier, placing an unidentified jet out at sea about a hundred miles off the coast. It had to be the one stolen by the invaders. It had dropped off the screen almost immediately, so they had no current bearing.

At Dolinsk to the south, a squadron of U-15s were lined up on the runway, their pilots awaiting orders. When the Foxhounds confirmed contact, they would go up, but only if the enemy was in their sector. The new aircraft had more sophisticated electronics. If anything in the sky could pinpoint the enemy, the Foxhounds could.

Sanchez passed out again as soon as Lee went aft. Russian voices were chattering in Barrabas's earphones—excited voices—probably searching for them. He switched to intercom and bellowed for Lee to get the hell back with the medic bag. If they couldn't raise Sanchez from his fog, they might as well say their prayers. There was no way he was going to land the crate alone.

Hatton arrived just as Barrabas was trying to make the turn again. They had to get the nose pointing south.

"Hang on, Lee!" Barrabas shouted as they started to lose altitude again. Precious air slid from the wings. The aerodynamics of the flight were being violated, and he didn't know what to do about it. He tried to haul back on the controls to get the wings level again. They were down to six hundred feet...five hundred...four hundred. At three hundred feet, barely above the heaving surface of the ocean, Barrabas leveled her out.

He looked at the compass. The bearing was almost right. They were heading south toward the Kuril Islands, still Russian territory, but closer to their goal. He eased the control bar back slightly, gave her power and they climbed to four hundred feet.

21

Colonel Kerensky was moving to his new assignment. The Foxhound had been refueled, and the tanker was hundreds of miles behind, dropping down to its base. He would make the trip from Moscow to Sakhalin in less than four hours, but even that was too long. Everything that could go wrong on Sakhalin had. He should be there now, directing the search.

"Get me Okha control again," he commanded the pilot.

This time, he had to wait for no more than ten seconds.

"Okha control."

"Is that Lomonosov?"

"Yes, Colonel." The sergeant's fear was evident.

"Patch me through to your flight leader."

"Yes, Colonel." The sergeant signed off, leaving only a hiss on the line to accompany the colonel's anxious thoughts.

"Red Flight Leader."

The transmission was faint. The colonel had difficulty understanding every word.

"This is Colonel Kerensky. Identify yourself."

"Red Flight Leader, Captain Meretskov."

"I'm the new KGB commandant for Sakhalin Island. I'm flying in from Moscow right now." He paused, letting the impact of his title and the dreaded image of the KGB sink in. "If you don't find and shoot down the commercial jet, you might as well fly out into the Pacific until you run out of fuel."

"Yes, Colonel." The answer came back without hesitation on the weak transmission. "I'd like some direction first, with all respects, Colonel."

"What direction, Captain?"

"The Korean incident made a lot of noise in our squadron, Colonel. If you want us to shoot down this one, we'll need a direct order, Colonel."

"Are you saying you will not obey my order, Captain?" Kerensky could feel the sweat roll from his armpits down the inside of his flanks. This assignment was going to be a bastard.

"No problem, Colonel. I will continue to hunt while you issue your orders to my base. If I get orders from the base to destroy, I'll destroy."

"Captain, you will obey my direct order."

"Colonel, with all respect, I received an order to scramble and wait orders to kill." Meretskov was in a hell of a bind. He had to protect his ass, but this man could make his life a hell on earth if he was for real—another Popolov. "I have not had those orders from my base," he continued. "I am not going to destroy a commercial jet and have the roof cave in on me as it did on my major last week."

"Dammit, man, you will..." The colonel stopped in midsentence. He was shouting into dead air.

THE OLD TUPOLOV FLEW ON, approaching the Kuril islands. Barrabas was sweating it out behind the controls. Lee Hatton was working over Sanchez, still trying to rouse the pilot so he could take over for the landing. Fifty miles behind, searching the Sea of Okhotsk, the squadrons of Foxhounds tracked their prey.

At the rear of the formation, Lieutenant Myatokin had listened to his captain and the unknown colonel argue. He had always been ambitious and was a hothead. And he had consumed almost a half bottle of vodka before they went up.

This was the chance he had been waiting for. The invaders had escaped. They were flying an old jet, trying to make it to a friendly nation. He pushed the twin powerplants to full power, pulled back on the controls and executed a climbing half roll that pointed the nose of his Foxhound toward Hokkaido.

The radar screen bathed the interior of Myatokin's proud beauty in a dull green. Within seconds he had left his patrol far behind. The lower end of the Kurils were stretched out before him.

Above the Kurils, he saw one lone blip heading toward Japan and safety.

NATE BECK WANDERED to the cockpit and sat in the engineer's chair vacated by Hatton. Idly he looked over the crude controls and flipped a switch. A small radar screen glowed light green, outlining the sea below and a long chain of islands. Ahead, he could see Hokkaido just coming into his screen. Behind, he could see a blip closing in on them—fast.

"We've got someone on our tail, Colonel," he said.

"Shit! What is it?"

"We'll know soon, Colonel—it's on us right now."

Barrabas had known they'd never be able to clear the area without being seen; they had lost the cover of darkness.

Movement to his left caught his attention. A wicked-looking fighter matched their speed. The pilot was gesturing.

"What's he trying to tell us, Nate?" Barrabas asked.

"You don't want to know, Colonel. He's shooting at us with his finger. A clown getting ready to shoot down another defenseless commercial jet."

Suddenly the Russian jet was gone.

"He's dropped back to fire a missile, Colonel. Did you see the armament on that son of a bitch?" Beck asked.

"What the hell was it, Nate?"

Their eyes were drawn to the right side. The interceptor had rolled over the top of them and was cruising beside them on the right.

"I think it's their newest," Beck said. "I accessed the Pentagon computer recently. That baby gives our people nightmares. Look at it! I think it's their Foxhound A. Two Turmanski R-31 motors can push it to Mach 2.4. They used to have four air-to-air infrared missiles. Now they carry eight radar-homing AA-9s."

"He has only four, Nate," Barrabas said.

"Right. They're not the new ones. He's carrying the infrared," Nate said. "Strange mixture. But Foxhound or Foxbat, we're just as dead."

"Maybe not," Barrabas said. "Have we got any phosphorous grenades left?"

"Shit, Colonel. We used every goddamned thing we had."

"Go back and see," Barrabas commanded.

The Russian had removed his helmet and moved in close. A satanic grin split his face as he raised one gloved hand and shot them down with an index finger. He threw back his head and laughed, then was gone.

Nate rushed back into the cockpit. "We have two," he said.

"Get back and open the rear door," Barrabas said. "When I shout 'Go' on the intercom, you pull the pin and toss one high and wide."

When Beck had gone, Lee turned to the colonel. "Is this going to work?" she asked.

"Who knows, Lee? I can watch the radar and see when the Russian lets one go back there. He has to drop back a couple of miles to avoid the debris."

"Nice choice of words," Lee observed.

"If we're lucky, the infrared will go for the grenade instead of our motors."

He turned to the radar, flipped on the intercom and yelled to Beck. "Get ready!"

A blip showed on the screen, but it was coming from the wrong direction. Barrabas didn't take time to analyze why. He yelled, "Go!"

The radar showed the Foxhound clearly. The next second it was gone. The grenade had been tossed and exploded behind them, but it had not stopped a missile. The Russian plane had just disintegrated, vanished into thin air.

"What happened, Nate? Did it work?" Barrabas shouted.

Nate poked his head into the cockpit. "The goddamnedest thing I ever saw, Colonel. One minute it was in the sky, and the next it was gone. I think I saw a cloud of debris, but I can't be sure."

"A defective missile?" Barrabas asked, holding desperately to the control column. He had not been able to break his concentration for a minute. The controls were acting strangely. He was sure some of the tail section had been shot off on takeoff. The whole thing could let go, and the plane would plunge them into the sea.

"It's possible. More like someone else shot him out of the sky."

The two men were alone in the cabin. Sanchez was still out of it. They glanced at each other, remembering other moments in battle that they had shared. Moments when they had been up against death.

"It's over, Lee," Barrabas called into the intercom. "Better come back to your patient."

CAPTAIN MERETSKOV HAD NOT CLAWED his way from the frozen wastes of Siberia to the Soviet airforce by being a fool. He had taken a risk in defying an order from an unknown colonel. He also knew his men. Myatokin was brash, boastful and had been drinking too much. He had broken formation. The damned fool was going after the enemy jet by himself.

"Red Flight to base," he called into his mike. "Red Flight to base."

"Okha base."

"Can you patch me with that colonel again?" he asked.

"Hold on, Red Flight."

Meretskov sat in the cockpit of his Foxhound, feeling sure that he had no other choice. He had not played the Soviet game of politics all his adult life without learning all the moves.

"I have Colonel Kerensky. Go ahead, Red Flight."

"This is Meretskov, Colonel. We have sighted your aircraft. I have dispatched one of my flight to shoot it down. Am standing by."

"You've just saved your ass, Captain. Call me when you have results."

"Over and out, Colonel."

THE ATTACKER FORGOTTEN, the Tupolov flew through bumpy air over the last of the Kuril islands as Barrabas gently eased her into the desired course a few degrees at a time. They were still at five hundred feet, less than fifteen minutes from the Japanese coast.

He looked over at Sanchez. The man's face was the color of the white clouds now curling into great puffballs over their heads. Lee was kneeling beside him again, passing salts, ammonia or something, under his nose. The Puerto Rican shook his head occasionally, but he hadn't really responded.

Looking down, Barrabas could see the fleet of ships bobbing in five-foot swells. He couldn't know that Tony Gray was still having bad dreams about the group he'd ferried to Mys Aniva not much more than forty-eight hours ago. He didn't know, and he didn't care. They had too much to handle now without thinking of the past. Not when the future was still uncertain.

He could see the tip of Hokkaido and knew they would have to make a course correction and an approach for an airport. He had to worry about what was ahead and what might be behind. With what they'd accomplished at Sakhalin, the Russians would probably not hesitate to shoot them down over Japan, especially if they had any idea of what they were carrying back. The Soviets wouldn't know about Popolov's confession and the videotapes, but they had to know their computer storage facility had been breached.

"How's Sanchez, Lee?" he asked as casually as he could manage. "We need him right now."

"I think he's coming around, Colonel. But no guarantees."

Barrabas had managed a few hundred more feet of altitude in the past ten minutes, but was afraid to lose it if he turned. He could see most of the northern coast of Hokkaido now. It was rocky and uninviting, no place for an inexperienced pilot to practice.

Sanchez had grunted a few times and opened glassy eyes, but was going to be little help. Barrabas searched the island below for a straight stretch where he might be able to crash land. God only knew what the result might be, but he had to do something. He was afraid of losing altitude if he had to make a wide turn.

He could see inland now. To his left, a major city pushed its buildings into the early morning sky. It would have to have some kind of airstrip.

He began to turn and immediately started to lose altitude. Four hundred feet from the ground, he decided he couldn't make it that way. He had to get the plane on the ground before the Soviets sent another of their interceptors after them, but he had to do it in one piece.

Sweat poured from his forehead and into his eyes. He was having difficulties seeing, and he couldn't take his hands off the controls.

"Lee! Get a cloth and wipe my eyes," he shouted to the doctor who was still working on Sanchez.

Lee Hatton heard the desperation in his voice and moved quickly. She took a clean swab from the medical bag and wiped away the sweat from the colonel's forehead.

He could see much better. He took the airplane up so he'd have some altitude to play with when he made his approach.

He coaxed it to a thousand feet. He could see the airport clearly. On three sides, tightly packed homes ringed the perimeter. A farmhouse and work buildings lined the other. Behind the farm buildings, ploughed fields lay bare.

As he tried the first tentative turn, he felt some resistance. The tail section had been damaged, and the controls hadn't been consistent, but this was something worse. If he couldn't correct the fault, they would plow straight into the houses ringing the airport.

In desperation he glanced at Lee to see how she was coming with Sanchez. The pilot was sitting more erect and had his hands on the controls. Lee met the colonel's eyes. She nodded.

Barrabas sat back, exhausted. He kept his hands on the controls to get the feel of the landing and watched Sanchez's practiced hands as he brought the plane around, eased off the throttles, gave her full flaps and lowered the landing gear. The plane seemed to sit in the air, a thoroughbred brought to heel, spirited, finely balanced, gliding gently toward the runway. He could barely see the farmhouse at the far end.

As suddenly as he had come around, Sanchez dropped off again. The nightmare continued. The surly beast yawed and fought Barrabas's hands. The tail shifted from right to left as they moved ever closer to the cement runway below.

They were a hundred feet up and a half mile out, then a quarter mile, three hundred yards, a hundred. The wheels touched the beginning of the runway, and they bounced twenty feet up into the air, came down and bounced up again.

Barrabas cut the engines and held on to the controls. He had no reverse thrust. Worse, he didn't know how to apply the brakes.

They flashed past the control tower, halfway down the runway, their speed undiminished. Barrabas stared, transfixed, his eyes on the farmhouse at the end of the runway.

The ribbon of cement disappeared. A stretch of muddy field separated the runway from the perimeter fence. When the undercarriage hit the mud, it collapsed. The nose plowed into the muck, and the cock-pit became a tomb, dark and forbidding, running a course to oblivion.

The plane carried fifty yards of chain-link fence into the farm property like a giant veil. It cut down a farm building with each wing, slid through a huge pile of cow manure and moved through the plowed field with the brown filth of the barnyard greasing the way to a smooth stop.

EPILOGUE

Nile Barrabas leaned back in the soft chair. He had a sandwich in one hand and a Japanese beer in the other. Sitting in overstuffed lounges and chairs, in the luxury of a Tokyo Sheraton suite, O'Toole, Hatton, Beck, Hayes and Nanos waited for a huge man to speak. The man was attacking a plate of German pastries with a fork. He had a spot of whipped cream on his cheek and a stream of cream running down his tie.

Through a mouthful of custard and puff pastry, Walker Jessup continued the debriefing. "Our people have already looked at Nate's tapes from the computer center. A great job there. We've been trying to get the specs on their new Foxhound A for a long time. It's a modified MIG-31 and a very hot item."

"What else was on the tape?" Nate Beck asked. He had seen it all on the console, but things had been pretty hectic at that time.

"Not really sure yet, Nate," Jessup answered, not stopping his assault on the pastries for a minute. "Looks like their newest missile cruiser and a nuclear sub the CIA had never even suspected. Just a great haul—lot of other stuff we haven't analyzed yet."

"What about our wounded?" Barrabas asked. "The last we saw, they were hauled out of the Tupolov and taken away by ambulance."

"Med-Evac took them out of Tokyo first thing this morning," Jessup replied, filling his mouth with a forkful of cream. "They should be halfway to the States by now. Taking them to Honolulu General, then on to the mainland."

"I'm not worried about Billy Two. He'll recover eventually," Barrabas said. "What about Sanchez? He did a bitch of a job for us. Last we saw of him, he didn't look good at all."

"Got a message he's going to be all right," Jessup said. He picked up a napkin and wiped his broad lips.

"I think I got most of it," Jessup went on, biting the end off a cigar and flicking a lighter. He blew smoke to the ceiling. "The computer center sounds like a total write-off. If we're lucky and the scientist Fedesoff didn't lie, they've got no backup. No way to analyze how bad they're hurt, but at minimum you set their research back about five years."

He blew smoke across the room and looked at each one in turn. "Looks like you did everything except what you were sent to do." He held up a massive hand to hold off comment. "We're grateful. The destruction caused by O'Toole alone was worth the trip. Very nice job all around, but . . . we wanted to know about the KAL thing."

The SOBs all looked at Barrabas. He motioned for them to leave the room. As they filed out in a line, he called after them, "Go out and have a couple of drinks. I'll see you at Omatu's in the morning for the payoff.''

Beck hesitated. The others waited, standing at the door.

''Do you know anything about a Foxhound disappearing off our tail, Jessup?'' Nate asked.

Jessup looked undecided for a few seconds, then seemed to make up his mind. ''Don't repeat this or it's my ass.'' He blew smoke at the ceiling and leaned back, looking up at the mercs who stared back at him.

''Last year, we built a secret base at Misawa on Honshu, about three hundred miles south of here. The President authorized us to keep F-16s ready all the time you were on Sakhalin in case they could help when you came out.''

He stopped to brush ash from the expanse of his stomach. ''The KAL thing really got to the President. He wanted to do something, you know? So a dozen pilots from Misawa kept up the vigil. They had a pool on who would get to shoot down a MIG. Your Foxhound, or whatever it was, didn't get off a shot.''

The SOBs were grinning. ''Thank them, okay?'' Beck said for all of them.

Jessup nodded.

When they were gone, Barrabas walked to the door of the suite and made sure it was closed. He passed in front of a puzzled Jessup, walked to a videotape deck he'd ordered from the hotel and pulled the Sakhalin tape from a pocket. He set the volume low and gestured for Jessup to pull his chair closer. He'd had Beck sweep the room earlier in the day. It was free from electronic eavesdropping. He didn't want the sound to carry beyond the four walls.

Jessup sat without emotion as Popolov was taken through the questions by Barrabas, who had stayed off-camera. When the screen went blank, the white-haired merc flipped off the set, then tossed the tape at a stunned Jessup.

"Anthony Jones Hopkins. Damn! Hard to believe." He sat back, blowing smoke to the ceiling. The place smelled like the smoking room of Jessup's club in Washington.

"What do you make of this Afghan thing?" he asked.

"I think it's a real threat," Barrabas said. "As I understand it, Popolov planted the idea with Persof's son and knew it would be passed on. He wanted General Persof to run with it and make a fool of himself."

"It doesn't matter who goes after the Afghan rebel leaders," Jessup said. "If they try it, we've got to stop them."

"Good luck with it." Barrabas got up to leave.

"Not so fast. I want your people ready to go in—now."

"No way, Jessup. They need rest and recreation. Maybe in a month. The Afghan thing doesn't go down for six weeks."

"All right. Keep in touch, Nile," the fat man said, pulling a sheaf of papers from his pocket.

"What's this?" Barrabas asked.

"Confirmation of transfers. The balance of the five hundred thousand to each of the SOBs' numbered accounts—less my 15 percent, of course."

"The accounts no one knows about." Barrabas grinned at him.

"The accounts no one *knew* about." Jessup grinned back. He tapped the ash from his cigar. "They don't call me the Fixer for nothing, you know." Jessup winked.

Barrabas took the papers from the Texan's paw, folded them carefully and put them into his breast pocket. He moved toward the door with a broad satisfied smile.

"Likewise for the SOBs!"

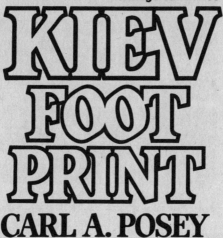

"An exciting, well-paced tale
of complex deception, fast action."
—*Chicago Sun-Times*

KIEV FOOT PRINT

CARL A. POSEY

Author of *Prospero Drill* and *Red Danube*

Miles above Earth, the space shuttle *Excalibur* floats lifelessly, its brave crew destroyed in a bizarre, unexplained accident. But as gravity slowly begins to reclaim the deadly debris, an on-board nuclear reactor transforms the crippled spacecraft into a lethal time bomb—a thermonuclear bullet locked on an unalterable course, aiming strait for the heart of Soviet Russia.

CATASTROPHE OR CONSPIRACY?

K-1